A

MW01681468

fierce harmony

ZEA KAYLEIGH GALAN

Fierce Harmony

www.zeakayleighgalan.com

For information contact :

zeakayleigh@gmail.com

First Edition: February 2026

To You,

Stand tall and never shrink yourself for their comfort.

There will be someone who treasures the safety of the shadow your greatness casts.

Listen to the Official Playlist

Victoria Monét — Alright
ATEEZ — All About You
Teddy Swims — The Door
Dhruv — double take
Bryson Tiller — Been That Way
Jackson Wang — Not For Me
ILY Ghoul — velvet wounds
Summer Walker — Session 32
Isaiah Falls — NIGHT OFF (feat. Sasha Keable)
Zara Larsson — Ruin My Life
SAILORR — CUT UP
Stray Kids — Unfair (Felix)
Elmiene — Light Work
Leon Thomas — Breaking Point (feat. Victoria Monét)
kwn — worst behaviour (feat. Kehlani)
Isaiah Falls — BUTTERFLIES (feat. Joyce Wrice)
Coco Jones — Here We Go (Uh Oh)
Lucky Daye — That's You

Listen on SPOTIFY!

Never miss an update about Zea Kayleigh, newsletter exclusives such as freebies and giveaways, first looks at new books, upcoming series, and events.

SIGN UP HERE!

A Thomas Family Novel

fierce harmony

Chapter 1

Lee Thomas

"This is not happening," I grumble, coming to a wobbly stop on the side of the road. There is, luckily, a service shoulder here, so I don't get flung from the side of the hill as people are passing by me.

Dropping to a crouch beside my bike, I stare at the offensive nail protruding from the side wall of my front tire. *Great.*

Fuck my life.

Exactly what I needed right now.

I rear back my leg as if I'll actually be able to follow through with kicking my baby. *Impossible.* Instead, I drop to the ground, uncaring of the leaves and clump of wet snow that is soaking through my jeans right now. I need to cool off.

It's Christmas.

And I'm stranded on the side of the Harmony Hills.

As if bad luck is meant to come in threes, I check my phone to find not one bar of service.

Fucking great.

My head meets the face of the stone behind me as I contemplate my options right now.

I've only got one good one—walk down the hill until I can get service to call a tow truck to come get me.

Crunching through snow, I'm inundated with the thoughts I was trying so hard to avoid by coming on a ride up here. Lately, I've been losing the comforts that I've been foolish enough to think wouldn't go.

A ride with the kind of scenery that painters could pour over for weeks just to capture will do wonders for mental clarity. How could you think about anything else when this is what awaits you?

Impossible.

But I'm *not* getting that beauty to distract me.

Nope.

I'm carefully and cautiously walking along the side of this highway in the cold, so that I won't be sideswiped by anyone on the road.

After walking down almost half a mile, I get my first bars of service to make my call to the local tow company.

I'm particularly adverse to small talk. I grew up in this town and my Mom was always making conversations with strangers and non-strangers, as one of the most well-liked people in our town.

Well, she did when she was alive.

Ever since her passing, I've hated it almost instinctively. If I can sense it coming, I avoid it at all costs.

That will not be a possibility for the next two hours...

This tow guy insisted on staying on the line until he could reach me—for forty-five minutes, by the way. Then talked all throughout loading my bike onto the back of his truck—an additional fifteen minutes. And finally thirty-five more minutes of him burning a hole through my ears with his yapping.

I don't know how many times I can say, "Wow, that's crazy." But everyone knows that's a blow-off response. He was not getting it. I wasn't listening, nor did I care.

He continued anyway, responding with, "No kidding. And do you know what I did..."

Heaven above, please tell me what I did to deserve this.

There isn't much time before I need to get ready for Christmas dinner now. I volunteered to have the meal catered since Thanksgiving was not only stressful for my older sister, Korra, but we had far more guests who showed up than anticipated. There was plenty of food, but I still think it's too much for one person to take on.

If Thomas family holidays are still going to be like one big open-door party, we should treat it as such—with catering.

I was able to get everything ordered basically right after Thanksgiving, so there was no difficulty in securing a spot for the next large holiday.

Showering quickly, and probably too quickly, I rub the contact right out of my eye... in the shower.

Yea.

It's gone.

At the clinic, I wear my glasses on a daily basis. I don't usually wear my contacts unless it's the weekend or when I'm going for a long ride on my motorcycle, which I haven't had a chance to do often.

That wouldn't be a problem except for the fact I have forgotten to order contacts for basically the last year. My last contact lens was probably well past the need to toss and replace. It is likely stuck to the shower wall or something, but I'd never know now.

Glasses it is today.

When I'm dressed, I have about fifteen minutes to pick up all this food from the caterer. It's a good thing that living in a small town affords me the ability to leave the house and make it there in time.

With the food loaded into the back of my truck, I make my way to my family's home. Snow caps the roof and standout turret at the front of the building that holds many of my childhood memories. With its forest-green siding and ivory trim, it paints a picturesque scene for what a Christmas story should be. Soft lighting glows from the windows, speaking to the life inside. As expected there are already a lot of people here. Luckily someone told them to leave the left side of the driveway open for me to pull in easily.

As I'm getting out of the truck, my older brother, Zach, is pulling in behind me. Rolling up the sleeves to my jacket, I call out to him. "Grab a few of these will you?"

His usual pleasant demeanor is unperturbed by the tedium of carrying these huge trays into the house. He had a long night of trying to suppress a holiday fire. Who knows if he got any rest at all after that, but he's still here on time when he could have taken more time to sleep. He doesn't complain as he grabs a few of them to follow behind me.

Walking up the path that leads to the short steps of the ivory porch is a little more tricky with the snow, but someone did a decent job of shoveling it. There is no need to get keys or anything out because my Dad's house is always unlocked. With a strong nudge to the front door it opens pretty easily.

The sound of chatter is already loud when I make my way inside. My first stop is the dining room to try and find my Dad amongst the people gathered and luckily I do.

He gives me a small smile of approval at the food in my arms, that grows larger with my older brother coming in behind me. *His real pride and joy.* A second born son doesn't come with very many perks, I'll admit.

My Dad stops Zach to talk with his guests, but doesn't mention my name.

Guess I'll drop this food off and go grab the rest of the trays.

I ask my sister's fiancé, Bryce Hampton, to help us get the rest of the food out of the truck since he's the only other man under the age of sixty in the room at present. Many of Harmony Hill's most respected businessmen are all gathered in this room that I haven't been invited to stay in. Taking note of that fact hurts just a little bit.

Bryce is already engaged in some sort of conversation with Wynn West. In his hand is a small kitten that he recently adopted. Her little tutu makes him look significantly less intimidating. Of the powerful men in this room, I'd say that the older man is one of the most threatening. Wynn is an attorney and legend in this town. He's been the only one ballsy enough to go against the Brenford family and win, more times than not.

Bryce appears grateful to be able to wrap up his conversation with Wynn to help me. He's also an attorney, but he works in big-time corporate law. After taking Wynn's card he hands off the kitten to Korra and helps me with the remaining trays.

I'm in the kitchen, making sure that the directions the caterer included with the food are followed to a T. I know for a fact that this food is going to have to feed lots of people. Though it may not be as delicious as something home-cooked by my sister or my Mom, it still needs to be done right.

I don't get an opportunity to finish preparing the food as necessary because bright red curls enter the room and my mood sours even more.

If that's possible.

Here is my third stroke of bad luck. Zadie McLane is here.

In Zadie's hands is a rather large tin container with Christmas trees and Labrador puppies with bows on them. Her charcoal-gray sweater that holds tight against her curvy figure briefly takes my attention off of my irritation in why she's here.

"Can I help you with something?" The question is harmless enough, however the tone in which I deliver it makes it very clear that I don't actually want to help her with *anything.*

McLane stands in my kitchen like she's welcome here. In any other circumstance, she probably would be. But in this one, where she has come to town after being gone for years to take my job—she's not.

She smiles, despite my unfriendly tone, "Yes, you could, *Bent.*" Her little extra emphasis on the nickname that I *do not use* is extremely irritating.

And she knows that.

She has been using it to get under my skin since we were in grade school and it still works. It's just as effective at pissing me off quickly as it was when we were in elementary, middle, or high school.

And like the idiot I am, I show her exactly how irritated it makes me by correcting her with the actual nickname that I use, "Lee." Moving to a different tray to assemble the rack and fuel cans for it, I ask, "What do you want, Zadie?"

Her smug face is happy to show me the festive cookie tin when she says, “Well, I baked some cookies. Do you already have a place for desserts in this humongous spread?” She gestures to the kitchen counters with the oversized racks holding the covered catering trays.

I didn’t have any actual desserts planned, no. Typically there are too many. People bring their own to these kinds of events at my family’s home. “You baked cookies? How do I know we can trust those?”

“I’d say that because they’re for the entire Thomas family and not just you, there’s no poison in them,” she responds with a tilt of her head to the left, exposing her soft neck and a bit of her collarbone from the neckline of her sweater dress.

Tossing the lids from the fuel can into the trash, I snark, “In that case, I’ll be sure to grab at least half of them to take with me.”

Her green eyes narrow. “You will do no such thing, especially because they will go perfectly with this.” She points a thumb to her side where I hadn’t noticed that she has her bag on her shoulder.

It’s been clear to me that Zadie has some sort of… wanderer's spirit. I don’t know what else to call it. She carries around a handbag, which more aptly resembles an overnight bag. Like at any point, she’s ready to just pick up and leave and never look back.

I honestly wish she would.

More than anything else, the thing is not organized in any sort of way. She can never find her keys or her phone. If you give her something and it goes into this bag—guaranteed you’re likely not to see it ever again. It has to weigh at least a ton. Don’t know how I missed that she had it to begin with.

Oh, right. The sweater dress and cookie tin combo.

From this bag, she pulls out a gallon jug of something.

“So, is this the poison?” I ask. The jug is a deep red and there’s lots of stuff floating in it that I can’t quite make out.

“Ha ha ha. Very funny, Bent. No, it’s not *poison*.” She mocks. “Though I probably wouldn’t recommend drinking too much of it. I made somewhat of an apple cider sangria.”

"*Somewhat*?" My face scrunches at the combination. "Apple cider sangria? What the hell is that? I'm pretty sure those things don't actually go together."

"Apple cider and wine definitely go together. Then put in some orange and some cinnamon sticks..." The look of whimsy lights her face. "It's delicious."

"I'm not letting you serve my family some drink you made in a toilet bowl that sounds like exactly where everyone's going to end up. Why are you mixing alcohols with a holiday?"

"It's come to my attention that you don't actually know what having fun is or what a good time looks like. Coincidentally, those two things are subjects in which I excel. So there are many reasons to mix alcohols on a holiday." She sets the gallon jug on the counter and begins moving around the kitchen looking for something. "Especially one like this where we're all eating good food. And by the looks of it, you've catered enough for us to live here for the next week. Over-compensating for something?"

Scoffing at her jab, I don't respond to it more than that. "What are you looking for?"

She doesn't answer me, instead making a sound of delight as she opens the cabinet that holds our glassware that isn't used as often. "These will be perfect," she says to the glass mug in her hand as she pours the first drink into it. "Just needs a cinnamon stick..." She pulls a container from the big purse and, of course, it has cinnamon sticks in it. "...and an orange." Yea. She has a container with sliced oranges, as well.

"Don't think you're going to get on Dad's good side by getting him drunk," I sneer as she prepares more of these questionable drinks. Not sure how I got here, but I've caged her to the counter so she can't return to the cabinet to get more glasses to pour.

Undeterred, Zadie garnishes the drinks she has poured and moves on to opening her cookie tin. All from the confines of my arms. Inside are sugar cookies shaped like stars with white icing decorating the top. "They look good don't they?" She teases as I eye the little star. "They're shortbread cookies. Melt in your mouth soft and a perfect compliment to my apple cider sangria."

She turns to face me, but I don't back away or give her more space. "Try some." She tilts her head again. "You know? To make sure that I'm not poisoning your family or whatever..."

I look down at the glass in her right hand and the cookie in the other.

Against my better judgement, I take both and step away from her. Biting into the cookie first, I'm disappointed that it does melt into my mouth. The buttery softness is just sweet enough to not be overkill with the icing on top. I try to keep my face neutral, not showing the enjoyment of her baked treat.

Dammit. It is good.

I want to take another bite, but I don't for my pride's sake.

Sniffing the drink for a moment, the smell of pomegranate, orange and apples are strong notes between the scent of cinnamon from the stick and the drink. I give it a sip anyway. *Oh, man.* That's even better than the cookie and she was right. They don't overpower each other.

Dammit.

I can't resist a deeper pull from the glass. It's warming and actually pretty delicious. You can barely taste the alcohol, which tells me right away that this is a dangerous drink.

"Good, huh?" She asks, smirk in place. She may as well reach over her shoulder to pat her own damn back.

I grunt instead of responding. There are still more dishes that need to be put on racks in the kitchen.

"I already know it is. I'll just be taking these with me." She snags the cookie tin from the counter, but leaves the drinks and the gallon of sangria. With another that has appeared on the counter as well. "Put those in the fridge won't you?"

Shaking my head, I do what she asks. If not to make sure no one else gets their hands on it. The last thing I need today is for the entire house to be buzzing off of her sangria and gushing about another thing she's better at than me.

My food will be the main event and her drink will definitely not be topping how I've taken care of the holiday.

At least, that's how I wanted it to be.

And as I should have known, everyone is a-buzz with their hands full. A drink in one hand and a cookie in the other before I know it.

Unfortunately, I am as well.

Dammit.

They were both too good.

I scowl at her from across the living room as most everyone has left for the evening. My sister and her fiancé started the exit procession and now only my baby sister, Nia, Zach and I are what remains of the Thomas family. Dad went to lay down about an hour ago. Zach's work friend, Gonzalo, and his daughter, Lucía, are here but it looks like they're on their way out with how sleepy Lucía has gotten.

And what do you know, Zadie sits across from me, legs folded up, barefoot on the recliner with a drink in her hand, talking with Nia who sits on a cushion on the floor beside her. Lucía has fallen asleep on Nia's lap with my sister running a calming hand over her curly hair.

"Think we're gonna call it. I've gotta use this down-time wisely if I hope to get her home and in bed without a fight," Gonzalo says.

Nia nods, shifting to set Lucía in her lap and then in her arms. "I'll carry her out."

The three of them leave and Zach throws up a hand, "Gonna go crash. It has been a long twenty-four hours. Goodnight," He says, wobbling up out of the room to the stairs.

With only the two of us left, the time of night has really caught up to me.

"How many have you had?" Zadie asks after a while of blessed silence.

Picking my head up from the back of the couch, I look at her through bleary eyes. I rub my eye underneath my glasses to make them work a little better. "Had of what?" I ask, only to irritate her. I know what she's asking and I'm not going to admit just how much of her sangria I've had.

She rolls her eyes before responding. "You know what. You look like you're moments from falling asleep. I'm about there myself and I've had four. Maybe this is the fifth...? Couldn't be sure."

"I'm just tired. It's been a long day." It's not untrue.

I still need to get my tire replaced on the bike, order more contact lenses and somehow figure out how I can qualify to get into the room with those men my Dad easily invited Bryce into. Not to mention, I'm still in competition for the vet position with the woman sitting casually across from me.

"Mmmhmmm," she hums. Unconvinced of my answer and from how heavy I feel, I'm sure it's obvious that I've had a lot. "Well, I'm not gonna be able to drive in the snow like this and Korra said I could sleep in her room..."

"Okay?" I ask, perplexed as to why she's telling me that.

"Her room is right across from yours..."

Again, I ask, "Okay?"

"Nevermind," she says, leaving the room with her giant bag in tow.

Going to bed isn't a bad idea actually. I'm not going to be able to drive home either.

With my legs heavy, I head upstairs to my childhood bedroom. My room is at the end of the haul, which is also the front of the house. Moonlight shines in the hall to give enough light to find my way, but Korra's door is also open with the light spilling out of it.

When I finally reach my old room, I don't know what makes me turn to the opposite doorway. But I do. Something draws me there, I don't know if it's a sound or just the energy. Either way, I'm looking at a sight I've not had before.

Zadie sits on my sister's bed in nothing but her lingerie. It's deep green and white lace hugging her body in all the right ways. Soft curves my hands are twitching at my sides to feel. Lush red curls spilling over her golden brown shoulders. Freckles dotting her smooth skin like constellations.

I don't want to be drawn, but dammit. I am.

"Close the door," she says and I do.

When did I get inside Korra's room?

"Okay," I respond, letting the door close with a soft click.

CHAPTER 2

Zadie McLane

"Sweetheart, you've lost your flow," my Mama says from behind me.

Staring at myself in the mirrored wall in front of me, I squat deeper to form the shape I know to be correct. "Can't get any deeper than this," I exhale, attempting to keep my breaths long.

She simply nods, moving around the room to help other people in the class.

What does that even mean?

"You're doing better than me," Korra huffs from beside me. She wobbles for a moment before Mama uses her foot to position Korra's back foot more accurately for Warrior Pose 2. "Thanks," she says.

From that point forward I do what I can to follow the sun salutation sequences and keep up with the overwhelmingly older patrons in Mama's class today. I think Korra and I are the youngest people here. This is cake. I've been doing Virabhadrasana II since I was five years old. But Mama is right.

My flow is off.

My body feels not my own and it hasn't since Christmas.

Inviting Bentley into bed with me was a great choice. Well, my body and little lady downstairs agree with me on that front. But my mind—not so much.

What was I thinking?

Not only is Bentley actually the most antagonistic person I know, but he's also been an extra large pill since I came back into town in September.

It's January and he's still pissed that we're working the same position.

Even if we weren't, it's always been a competition to him. In school we were on the same debate teams, honor societies, and often had to work against each other for the purpose of making the other stronger. He never was a gracious loser and I'm no slouch. If I'm better, I'm not going to forfeit just to spare his feelings.

Needless to say, Bentley Thomas has been a thorn in my side since forever.

It's absolutely unfortunate that he grew up to be an irrationally attractive guy who's chip on his shoulder is even more attractive to me now more than ever.

Ugh.

I have got to resolve the attraction I have to toxic qualities that lure me in. I wish it weren't that way though it is.

Years of traveling abroad haven't made my taste in the opposite sex any better.

Seven countries I've lived in since I was twenty-two and I can count on my hand the number of men that I could actually see myself with long term. I don't think I even need my hand for that because it is zero.

Dating is about as fruitful as buying fruit at a farmers' market. You better use it quickly to get the best benefits or it all spoils… and then spoils everything else around it.

No offense to farmers' markets.

All offense to the garbage men I've been with.

In normal circumstances, I would talk to a friend about how off I've been feeling. Or better yet, move on because I know my stay is only temporary in the grand scheme of things.

This isn't normal circumstances though.

I returned to Harmony Hill because I want to put down roots. I want to belong somewhere again. Sure, I loved traveling. I loved exploring, but nothing ever felt close to home like the Hills.

This fact doesn't sit well with me since I left on the strength of finding my fit. Returning feels like I gave up. This town is the same as it's always been, though I'm even more different than I was when I left.

With my hands under my shoulders and pelvis hovering over the mat beneath me in a Plank pose, I'm forced to lock eyes with myself in the mirror again. My yellow athletic tank top and leggings look especially good in this pose. Like this mat, they have been with me to several countries and still look best in Mama's studio.

You deserve to be grounded, Z.

"Take one more inhale here, using your breath to find a natural flow of your own to complete the sequence again," Mama guides the class and I do as she has instructed.

I focus on my breathing and listening to my body's needs as I finish out the class. After the lowered lights are returned to their normal brightness, I'm still lying on my back in Corpse pose when Korra stands over me.

Half of her coils are clipped up and out of the way, but I don't miss the slight sheen of sweat at her temple. "I needed this today. How long has it been since I've worked out?"

"I do recall a nearly six-mile hike you went on for the most epic proposal I've ever heard of..."

She goes a little ashen at the reminder. "Bryce would have never heard from me again if the views and ring weren't as amazing as they are." She flushes, cheeks growing warmer. "That man had me sweating through my ears and he just casually walked up." With a sigh, she sits down beside me. "Worth it though," her eyes twinkle and she looks down at her ring finger.

"I told you he didn't look like he needed any training," Finally deciding to get up, I roll up and through my spine to a sitting position. "One day I'll be lucky, I guess. Until then, I'll just keep intimidating all the men I know."

"Not true. Zadie! You're such a catch. Your guy is out there. I know it."

With her words, my mind draws up memories of Bentley's strong back under my fingertips, and then it self-corrects to a memory of him ignoring me in the clinic when I tried to tell him I had already taken the Poodle back because he was busy.

My head is all kinds of messed up right now.

Korra would be the first person that I talked to about my problem with Bentley except for the fact that—he's her brother. I love the Thomases, but they cannot keep secrets from each other. I don't want anyone to know that Bentley and I hooked up. *Especially Korra*. Her idealistic outlook on the world is not particularly beneficial for my delulu that I can somehow fix that chip Bentley has.

Instead of spilling my guts, I say, "Sure, he is. Until then, I've got my completely parasocial relationship with an idol who touched my hand when I lived in Korea. We're going to be happily married," She chuckles to which I add, "Me and about two million of his other fans."

She shifts over, bumping my shoulder with hers. "Well, I never did picture you for the jealous type."

We laugh together, finally getting our things packed up to leave.

A group of women are talking with Mama by the door on our way out. I recognize Joyce and Marina but the other woman, I'm not familiar with. She introduces herself though my mind is already distracted by my Mama's expression. Korra easily fills the space of my absence because Mama is scrutinizing my person.

Brenda McLane is not a confrontational person, which suits teaching Yoga and Pilates just fine. But it does not suit when she has something on her mind that she thinks might upset me. Even her saying that I had lost my flow earlier could be considered a jab by her standards.

Call me riled up, because I step aside with her arm in my grasp. It's not a strong pull, but I am tugging her for an aside. "What's going on?"

"I don't know what you mean," she says, brushing a stray curl up and into my high bun.

"You do," I insist, placing a hand on my hip. "What did you mean by me losing my flow before?"

Discomfort is a living thing on her normally content face, "Princess, I meant nothing by it. There is just a tightness in your body that isn't common. You're following the motions, but not feeling it. You know?"

"No," I respond drolly. "If I'm making the shapes, then I'm doing the practice." I adjust the yoga mat on my shoulder to sit more comfortably across my back.

"Yoga is not about making the shapes. You know this. Yoga is about connection. Connecting mind to body and body to spirit. That can be different, look different, each day." She shifts on her feet. "Have you tried outdoors since you've been home?"

"No?" I say, raising an eye brow. "It's freezing outside. I have no desire to catch a cold."

"One practice would not kill you, my love. Besides, you could do it at home in the sun room."

At my parent's place, they have an add-on to the original house with glass ceilings and minimal flooring. It has to be maintained like a garden, but it comes with the benefit of being able to actually touch grass or ground to the earth in your asanas or poses.

I haven't tried to find any comforts in living at home again because I desperately want to move out. I've been much too preoccupied with work and, I'll be fair, exploring the beauty of Colorado since I've been back stateside. There really is so much to do here and I hope to find all the good things in my weekends. Leasing a place of my own or, *gasp*, buying a home is just a little too much commitment right now. My free soul still needs time to jump into that just yet.

Mama reaches for the hand I've put on my hip. Her brown skin contrasts my own golden brown when she brings our clasped hands to her lips. "Don't be offended by my words. It was simply observation. You have not lost something that was not yours to own. You'll find your flow when you are ready."

Her words are meant to comfort, but I don't feel reassured. Instead I feel like it's time for me to leave and fast. "Okay, Mama," I say, with a kiss to her cheek. "Korra and I are going to go. I'll see you at home."

The words make me feel like the lost child I was in school, but I carry on to rescue my friend from small talk so that we can get out of here.

With our coats and boots on, we walk down Main Street to the restaurant for lunch. If I didn't suspect that Korra really wanted to go back to her apartment to care for her plants, I would have suggested we eat somewhere more scenic. There is a small café nestled into the side of the Hills that I've been dying to get back to. From the window of the restaurant we can still see the Harmony Hills, but it's not as nice.

"Is that Lee? Where is he going?" Korra asks when the sound of his motorcycle picks up and dies off as he parks across the street.

His signature red bike is a giveaway of who the driver is before he takes the helmet off. His curls spring into place after rubbing a hand over them and setting the helmet on the handle. Living in this tiny place gives him the luxury of not having to even lock that thing away.

Why does such an infuriating man have to look that good in jeans? *I wish he'd stop working out.* I mean the taper from his shoulders to that stupid little waist is aggravating in the extreme. I have to correct how I'm biting my lip before his sister catches me doing it.

The both of us are nosy. We're watching him walk towards town hall. I hold my breath waiting to see exactly where he is going but he ends up going to the bar that butts against it on the right instead.

"Maybe I should have invited him to have lunch with us..." Korra muses, taking a bite out of one of her chips.

Korra has seen the two of us bicker or simply ignore the other's presence at work since she works the front desk for Thomas & Friends Veterinary Clinic. And frankly, she caught it when we were growing up as well. Though I was, technically, in the same school year as Bentley, Korra and I are the same age. Korra and her twin sister, Kasey, were a year ahead of us. I'd hang out at her house and inevitably run into him and his equally unfunny friends when we were younger. He couldn't best me at school but with his friends on his side, he definitely tried to talk whatever shit he could. It was more annoying than anything else and I think I still had better comebacks than he did.

As adults, you would think that the bickering had come to an end.

You would think that after Bentley and I had sex, that the bickering would come to an end.

One might infer, but one would be wrong.

“Yea... maybe,” I say, mind and body still feeling off after a night I can’t take back.

Chapter 3

Zadie

I am the definition of a girls' girl. Okay? I love to see other women winning.

Especially someone like Korra.

So, with her announcement at the Thomas family dinner table, I couldn't be more excited for her. Though being in this house is a little uncomfortable with my new memories associated with it.

Christmas was almost a month ago and I've moved on.

She's always been the friend that puts herself last and really—she puts herself last in this family, too. The Thomases love the Thomases, but I'm positive that she loves them more. I'm pleased that she is getting the life that truly makes her happy.

Bryce seems like the type to make sure she is. My friend is beyond lucky and he certainly hit the jackpot with her.

Sunday nights, they all get together to have dinner. I don't normally join them, but Korra invited me after Yoga the other day.

My boss, Wayne, responds to the news that Korra and her fiancé have just shared with all of us gathered here. "Set a date? Bought a house? This is all wonderful news." His aged face, though not truly telling of how old Wayne is, wrinkles in worn lines of happiness for his daughter.

I squeeze Korra's hand from my spot next to her. "Oh, that is so good! Congrats you two!" I look around in my purse for my phone, but I am not feeling confident that I'll find it this time. "Someone call Nia."

"Already on it," Kasey says. Nia, the youngest Thomas sibling, picks up immediately and is both impressed and excited about the news Korra's sharing.

We're all startled by the front door slamming, interrupting the good vibes that we've been enjoying. There is only one Thomas currently missing from the table, so it's not hard to decipher that Bentley is about to come in here to stir up some shit.

Long, internal sigh.

I begin discreetly putting my things away. I'd like to leave before he goes into a full blown tantrum. That chance is long gone when his voice precedes him into the dining room.

"Why would you invite her here?" Bentley booms into the space. "Don't I see her enough as it is?"

Well, I can't say that I'm surprised by his sentiment. Our circumstances aren't ideal and I, for one, am not particularly happy to share so much time with him either. It isn't my fault that Korra and I are friends or that he has been an oversized pout at work, making everyone else uncomfortable.

I'd feel bad for him if he weren't such an ass all the time.

Giving up on escaping quietly, I take the extra-large claw clip I found in my purse when I was looking for my phone to pull my curls out of my face. When I was younger I had a habit of hiding behind them. Now, I do no such thing in the face of adversity. "Relax, *Broken*. I can be friendly if you learn to use your indoor voice. What's with the yelling?"

I know why he's yelling or at least part of the reason. Doesn't mean that I shouldn't have my own fun poking at the growly bear who is currently hulking behind his chair. I do mean *hulking* as his shoulders rise in tandem with his heavy breathing.

The open seat is still empty while he decides if he will sit or not. Kasey and Zach have both moved their things over to give him more space on the table, more out of habit I'm guessing. If he really didn't want to be here with me then he should have turned around when he saw my ride. The yellow SUV is a dead giveaway and the first thing that likely set him off.

His jaw ticks at my intentionally incorrect nickname. From behind clenched teeth, he snarks, "Don't you have your own family? Must you infiltrate mine?" He finally takes a seat and grabs food from the table.

Wayne interrupts our bickering before it can begin, saying, "Lee, watch your mouth. You're acting like a child. Zadie is always welcome in this house."

The overachiever in me preens at the support from my boss. But, I still wince at his remarks about Bentley being a child, which he absolutely is being, but—yikes!

Bentley doesn't take the admonishment and continues running his mouth. "This woman has come to take the position that I've been working my whole life to have. She bounces in here with her 'sirs' and smirks. Now, she's welcome where I'm meant to have at least some reprieve from work stress? You don't care about me at all! What's up with that, *Dad*?" I don't understand the tone in which he says Dad but I don't need to. This is not my fight.

When Zach joins in, I can't help but feel a little sorry that I've increased the upset that Bentley was feeling. "Okay, this dinner is not about either of you. It's for the family. Do I need to send you both out of the house?"

I was just on my way actually.

Glaring at Bentley, I say, "You know what? I'll go," seeing this as the opportunity that I needed to get away from this situation.

My attempt is thwarted again when Wayne stands. "No one is leaving. I'll clear this up right now. Yes, I did bring Zadie in because she's qualified and will be an amazing addition to the clinic if we're lucky enough to keep her. The decision to leave my life's work is a hard one to make, but I need to know that there is someone who can fill my shoes and make me proud."

My jaw drops. There is no way that he is going to do this here where all of Bentley's siblings can hear. I cannot fathom how I'm supposed to behave with the escalation of Bentley's tantrum being Wayne putting him in his place.

"Tonight is a perfect example of why I have my doubts about it being you, Bentley. I'd been vague before but at this rate, you are making the choice to promote Zadie even easier. My legacy is about more than following procedure. It's about ethos." It takes effort, but I manage to close my mouth when Wayne gestures toward me. "You disrespect our guests, a colleague. You have a bad attitude with staff. You've been a loaded cannon, ready to blow at any point. That is not the Thomas way."

Smoke is coming out of Bentley's ears when Wayne addresses me directly. "I'm sorry that you were made to be part of this problem, Zadie. I wouldn't blame you for wanting to go. If that is what will make you more comfortable, I won't hold it against you."

I can't stay after everything that was said at this table. It's far too awkward for even me to stand. I appreciate Wayne sticking up for me—hell, rooting for me—but I would rather not be here to make this worse. "It's alright, sir. I should probably get going anyway. Thank you for dinner," Wayne doesn't speak his agreement but nods.

Hefting my bag onto my shoulder, I hug Korra, wishing her and Bryce congratulations again. On the momentum of a goodbye to everyone else at the table, my exit is uninterrupted. Stuffing my arms into my coat, I high-tail my ass straight to Lemon and throw my purse into the passenger seat.

In the quiet of my cabin, I can breathe for a moment. I need to process what just happened before I get on these snowy roads. A distracted driver is not a safe one. My thoughts are complicated and layered with questions.

I feel like a coward sitting in my SUV. And then even more stupid for still recalling what it was like when Bentley wasn't such a prick to me.

When he looked at me in that doorway, I felt like a prized possession. Like a trophy with how his eyes glimmered. *Maybe it was just the alcohol.* For someone who has such a foul temper, he was a gentle lover. Not just gentle but attentive and responsive to my needs. The glaring contrast between *that man* and the one who I just left in the dining room is unbelievable.

I had found out from Korra and Kasey talking last week that his ex dumped him. I didn't know why, but I didn't need to. I was the rebound in some regard. Not emotionally, that's for sure, but physically. Neither of us were ready to take what we shared there out of the bedroom but the fact that his ire has somehow increased since then is mind-boggling.

I mean what was that? All because I was there for a Sunday dinner? The Thomases often have guests on Sunday so I don't see what the problem is.

My head falls to the steering wheel where I recount what Wayne said. I could become the vet on site. Promoting me to the position that I know Bentley has wanted his whole life would likely send him into a full on tailspin.

None of which excuses his behavior. You know this, Z.

There's a tapping on my window that startles me for the second time tonight.

Pulling my head from the wheel, I turn to see Bentley standing there with brows pulled down over his light brown eyes. I debate on whether I should reverse out of the space. Going as far as pressing my ignition start button and shifting into gear. When he looks as if he believes that I will actually leave him standing there, I roll my window down to an expression that's morphed from its original grimace.

"What do you want, Broken?"

He doesn't bother correcting me, instead he simply says, "I'm sorry for how I acted back there. It was uncalled for."

"Oh," I respond, too shocked to believe that he's actually apologizing. "I, um, accept your apology." My words barely leave my mouth before he adds more to this apology I should have seen right through.

"But I would prefer it if you didn't come to my family's house any more," he says with a straight face.

"What?" I blink at him several times. "You can't ask that of me. I'm—No. I'm not going to stop coming over."

Bentley pleads with his eyes. "Why can't you give me this one thing, Zadie?"

He doesn't often address me by my name. Though I tease him and call him all kinds of nicknames, he hardly ever says mine.

Except for that night...

"Completely silly of you to ask me that. Korra and I are friends." I shake my head. "She's my best friend and I was *invited*. Not just by her either." I don't have to elaborate for him to recall how Wayne extended the invitation.

His breath is a visible thing in the winter night. With the street lamp illuminating his face in a golden glow, I can see his jaw tick as he grinds his teeth. "Look, it's just not a good time. Alright? I'm not saying forever, but I need time to have something of my own. You understand?"

"No," I snap. "I don't. You have your own condo to yourself. There is plenty of alone time you can have."

"I know I'm alone there! You don't think I know how much alone time I have?" His voice rises when he responds. It's jarring and I flinch. Lemon rolls back ever so slightly. Though he always has something snarky to say, he rarely raises his voice at me.

I shift my SUV back into park and cross my arms over my chest. I don't know where his influx in general irritation is coming from, but I do my best to de-escalate the situation. "Look. I'm sorry about your break-up. It's hard to go through something like that, especially over the holidays. But—"

"What would you know about Malaya? Have you ever been in a relationship longer than a month? That would require you to stay in one place wouldn't it?"

His words hit me harder than I was prepared for.

"I see you weren't really sorry about how you acted back inside." My eyes prick with tears, not realizing how raw that wound was. "If making me feel unwanted was your goal, you've made your point. I won't be granting you the benefit of not seeing me everywhere you look, *Broken*. Consider *this* your warning that I'm prepared to see it through to the end."

Before, I felt bad that working at his family's clinic put him in a bad spot. I had even felt badly that Wayne was considering giving me his role over Bentley.

But now, I have no such feelings.

I'm not someone who will ever be overlooked or treated this way by anyone. Especially Bentley when we have no reason for the animosity.

He wants a fight, then he's in the wrong weight class stepping into the ring with me.

This spoiled nepo baby will be put right in his place.

His brows slam down over frustrated eyes. "Fine," he says, not waiting for a response from me. Instead he stomps over to his own truck, reversing and heading down the street away from the turmoil he's caused in me.

Chapter 4

Lee

The room is tense with silence as I eat my food unbothered by the awkward vibe now that Zadie has left. "What?" I ask when I feel all their eyes on me.

"Okay, I see what you mean by Lee wanting to be punched." Nia says, still on speakerphone. "I'm disappointed, big brother."

I'm the closest to Nia and it stings to hear her say that on the back of what my Dad has said to me tonight.

Zack takes my plate. "You need to apologize to her. You were beyond rude. What the hell was that?"

"I'm not." I say, leaning back in my chair. "She's a big girl. She's fine."

"Look, I know you've got a lot on your plate right now—" Korra says.

"Is that supposed to be funny?" I ask, still without the plate of food I made for myself.

Korra speaks again, this time with Bryce rubbing her arm in encouragement. "No, it's just an expression. Lee, you're better than this. Whatever you're going through, we're here to support you. This is not the way. I know you're hurting. Hurt people hurt people. You're stronger than your doubts. Taking it out on Zadie is not the way."

Grinding my teeth, I stand from my seat. "Fine. I'll go after her, but it won't be to apologize." They have their opinions but I leave them in the dining room.

Ripped away.

The sound of it rings in my ears as I drive away from my family's home to my condo. The drive isn't long, but the thoughts of every loss Zadie represents sits in the passenger seat beside me along the way.

How dare Zadie?

How dare she come back to Harmony Hill?

How dare she apply for my job?

How dare she make drinks that make me lose my rational thinking?

How dare she look like temptation and pull me under like a siren?

How dare she refuse to leave my head?

How dare she threaten to take what is my birth right?

Of all the answers I've been seeking on my own, there is one that stands in contrast to the others.

I don't have a birth right because the only parent I know is gone.

When my Mother died last year, she took the truth to the grave with her.

After Christmas, I went to help my siblings pack up our Mom's studio. Delanna Thomas was a saint. A music teacher and talent, she brought light to everyone she came across in Harmony Hill and beyond. She was a pillar in this community. She was the anchor to keep everyone in this family exactly where they were supposed to be.

Years of being the youngest son was never an issue that could go far because my Mom didn't play favorites with her children. If anything, my siblings would say that she did with me. I got away with more than I likely should have because my Mother was gentle and positive in her parenting of all of us. Me, included.

But I wasn't *unaware* of how I was different from Zach, Korra, Kasey and Nia. My siblings were exactly what half of Wayne and Delanna would look like.

My twin sisters mirrored each other and my mother. Deep skin and tightly coiled hair. Wide smiles and little round noses.

But my Dad was most visible in Zach and Nia's faces. They look like a triplet set. Big deep brown eyes, the same color of their skin, broad noses and full lips. Though both went through what they called an *ugly phase*, they both grew up to look just like Wayne.

Either way, you could pick out the features from each of our parents on any of them.

Me?

I could always find Mom in my looks. I had her nose and her coils. She would say that I got her talent and found peace in music like she did.

But other wise, I didn't look like them, my siblings. My skin was lighter, an ochre brown instead of the deep sable like Delanna or Wayne. My face was dissimilar. I was always aware of it. Spending more time in the sun, avoiding my sunscreen from time to time so I could tan a deeper shade... There was nothing I could do outside of that. It was clear that I was not like them.

But then Korra found something in that studio that changed everything. I was playing a song that Mom used to love on her piano when talk of a man I didn't know came up. Korra had found a bloody neck tie that was wrapped around an ID from the Brenford Mill in Mom's things.

I can't explain how goosebumps skated over my skin when I saw the ID. There was no way that I couldn't see what was plain to me.

This ID card from Aiden Kindrick, a man I never met, somehow looked more like me than I did. Though the photo was grainy from time, the person smiling in that photo was *important*. I had to know that it would be so. How could I not?

My siblings had all seen the ID before me and couldn't see me reflected in Aiden Kindrick's face. I'd seen it immediately and it affected me so deeply that I reacted in the only way I felt was appropriate. At once, I wanted to go and question my Dad. Try to find out everything that I could since he had to know something. *I know he did.*

But Zach held me back and Korra reasoned that it was a bad idea.

They thought that it was a bad idea for me to find out if this man, from an ID that my Mom had kept hidden away for my whole life, was my birth-father. And I had listened because I didn't know if I could handle any more revelations.

My resolve lasted for about one week. The fear of the unknown was eating at me all the while.

I tried to look for this man, but he was long dead.

The two people who I knew so adamantly were my birth parents were both dead. *And I was pissed.*

Everyone had lied to me. I didn't know just how many people had.

Was it just Mom and Aiden?

Did Dad know too?

Why was I never told the truth of my birth?

And the man who I had called Dad my whole life, wanted to take what was left of my worth away from me. He wanted to give Zadie my spot.

Never mind that I had looked up to him my whole life.

Never mind that I had pursued veterinary medicine because he was my hero.

Never mind that his legacy was one that I earned the right to continue.

Never mind that he was the only parent I had left.

Then, here comes Zadie. The girl who easily bested me in school. The world traveler who, even in her absence from Harmony Hill, still garnered gossip about where in the world she was next.

Was she in Belize? Or maybe she was in Ireland now. Better yet, she sent a photo from the mountains in Korea. Morocco then Cape Town? Of course. Maybe she'll be in New Zealand for the foreseeable future.

Ugh.

Who cares about any of that stuff when she still ends up back in Harmony Hill? She thought she was better than all of us and still, she's the small town girl anyway.

I don't care who she is.

I won't let her take my place.

Sitting on the couch, I debate whether it's worth it to make something to eat when I've long lost my appetite. I hadn't taken anything off when I got home. There's texts waiting for me when I pull my phone out of my coat pocket. Still furious about how the night went.

Scrolling past the texts from my family, I see my ex's text and grind my teeth. Pretty soon I won't have any teeth left.

Malaya: I'm moving next week. Either you come and get your stuff from my place or I'm donating it to a shelter.

Another loss I would rather not think about, but I can't ignore her anymore.

Malaya had been my girlfriend for three years. When she moved here, I met her at the clinic with her cat, Trixie. It wasn't a connection or anything right away but Harmony Hill being the small town it was, I ran into her more and more and eventually asked her out. She's funny and bold but also hard working. We had a lot in common and for a while I thought she was going to be the woman I married.

But I'd made a mistake.

Shortly before Thanksgiving, I had let it slip that I'd had a vasectomy. It was routine and I had no issues with the procedure. But she was livid that I hadn't talked to her about it beforehand.

I don't regret having it done at all. I don't want to have kids. And instead of having a slip up, I took care of the issue. *Pretty logical thinking if you ask me.*

Malaya didn't agree.

She wanted a big family. She didn't have siblings growing up and she wanted something different for her life. Malaya really didn't know what she was asking for. Somehow we had never had a real conversation about children together.

It was a mess, alright? The whole thing was one big explosion that ended with her leaving my condo and taking her things with her.

I'm sad but hey... I wasn't going to budge on the *kids thing*. There was no compromise and I can't blame her for standing her ground either. It was probably best that she left, but maybe not in this way.

It's no secret that everyone thinks I'm an asshole. But I didn't think that making this choice would make me apparently *the biggest selfish asshole she knew*. Her words–verbatim.

Lee: Donate them then.

Tossing my phone on to the couch, I finally get into the shower and ready for bed. In flannel pants, I pad over to my piano and take a deep breath. On the exhale I begin playing a song. It's the one that my Mom liked. I never did finish it before the reveal of that necktie occurred.

It doesn't take long before I lose myself in the song. John Legend's words flow from my lips and it's as if I can hear my Mom's praise from just behind me again. Her harmonizing with her favorite parts.

"*You deserve it all...*"

My eyes burn, but I keep playing, opting for something more somber.

Letting the words flow from me, I sing, "*luck will leave you cursed, it is a faithless friend*," the lyrics resonating like never before from Michael Bublé.

I play more music that reminds me of Mom until my back is stiff and my fingers ache, then flop into bed.

I was invited. Not just by her either.

Zadie never cared about being at my house—Unless it was to rub in my face how she was doing better than me at just about everything we were both participating in at school. As teenagers, I would be more frustrated that there were always so many girls in the house. Between my studying to get ahead, and the snickering of so many female voices, it was infuriating. I had to ignore it or counteract by bringing friends of my own over. It was difficult to study and even more difficult to bear knowing that she was able to relax and I was still behind. It just made me want to work harder and be better.

I won't be granting you the benefit of not seeing me everywhere you look, Broken.

What she doesn't know is that even with her trying to stay out of my way, she'd never be out of my head. She's too tangled amongst all the complicated commotion already present.

CHAPTER 5

Zadie

"You have to go inside, Z. This is your job regardless if your boss's son is, both, annoying and attractive. The annoying part far outweighs the attractive part. Give. Him. Hell."

Ugh.

I press my forehead to the steering wheel for another minute before finally getting out of Lemon. I'm fifteen minutes early for my day though I had to have a heart-to-heart with myself before entering the building.

As I'm opening the door, the sound of Lee's truck pulling up behind me sets my nerves on edge.

Could I not have been able to make it inside?

My luck is just not that good, I suppose.

I hurry inside anyway, unwilling to let him know that I've noticed him at all. Setting my coat on a hanger in the closet, I smooth the hair by my face back one final time though the curls there don't listen anyway. I'd taken time to make two French braids today. It is basically my equivalent to a game face. People tend to think that the curls make me more personable or just friendly, I guess.

I don't want any cuteness confusing my mission.

We hates Bentley Thomas.

No cuteness for him.

Bentley shuffles in, giving me no space when he reaches for a hanger of his own to hang his coat on. I could just move out of the way, but I'm not allowing him to think that I wasn't serious before.

With my arms crossed over my chest, I stand my ground. It feels petty, but would it have killed him to wait for me to finish putting my things away?

His head tilts, recognizing the challenge. "Okay, then," he says, taking the initiative and walking to the other side of the small coat room.

Korra comes into the room next, unaware of the tension between Bentley and I. She hangs her own coat, telling me about the patient I missed yesterday, who had gotten into a bag of Valentine's Day candy. She hooks an arm under mine and continues sharing her story as we walk into the clinic.

I have Mondays off since there are two lead techs at the clinic now. Bentley has Fridays off since I was trying to be somewhat gracious of the situation before. It was honestly the same either way since we both had a three-day weekend. Thank goodness I didn't have to be at work directly after what happened after dinner on Sunday.

I needed the extra day to recuperate and calm down. I'm not one to let things get under my skin but this entire Bentley situation is twisting me up more than I'd like to admit. No amount of Supported Child's pose could settle the stress I'm dealing with.

If Korra can sense how I'm on edge today, she doesn't show it. "We've got a few friends on the schedule, so I'm gonna head up front while you get the machines set up. Dad's coming in late today."

This update piques my interest. "He is?"

"Yea, he really does enjoy his off-time," she admits. "I think it's only a matter of time before he fully steps down."

"And chooses Bentley to take his place..." I hedge, mostly because I'm keen on knowing whether all he said was a bluff at Bentley's expense or if he truly might give me the role over his son.

She shrugs. “I wouldn’t be so sure. After dinner last weekend, I think it’s pretty clear that he’s leaning towards promoting you.”

“There is no way that Bent would work under me.”

“Please choose a better way to say that,” she giggles, covering her ears. “I had *the worst* image in my head. Yuck.”

With her words, it makes me recall a memory of Bentley working under me and it isn’t the worse...

But it is completely unwelcome.

The man in question walks past us to the testing room.

He will not be getting there before me.

“I’m gonna get to work, but I do appreciate the vote of confidence.”

“Sure,” she says, but I’m down the hall to the testing room before she can say more.

“What do you think you’re doing?” I ask when I see he’s pressing buttons on the machine that he shouldn’t be touching.

“Running background...” He points to the screen that shows what function he’s running on the chemistry machine.

“I can read,” I snarl in his direction, looking around for anything that he might have missed in trying to out-do me. “But that’s my task for the day. I’m Tuesday, Thursday, Friday.”

He raises an eyebrow, crossing his arms as he leans on the counter’s edge. His arms make the hem of his scrubs sleeves tighten. “So what? It needs to be done and I was free,” he says.

I cross my arms in turn. “Why? Your Dad’s not going to be here ’til noon. There’s no one to impress.”

His smile is smug as he takes in my irritation. “The simple fact that you know you’re slacking is reward enough for me.”

“It’s not slacking. I’m here to do it now.” My pager dings with the first patient of the day. “Never mind. Look, I’m taking the first client. So just, back off.”

He holds his hands up. “Sure thing.”

In a huff now, I take a few moments to calm myself and put on a smile for whoever is waiting in the lobby for me. I’m thankful that the first pup I bring back for the day is one who just needs an ear cleaning. It's not the worst set of ears I've ever seen, but they are in dire need of some TLC before it becomes a problem.

"Winston is not this calm with me. If he were, I wouldn't be here," Celena, Winston's owner, says from the other side of the table I'm working on. "You probably think I don't care about him at all."

"Just the fact that you brought him in, is proof enough that you love him. The maintenance is the biggest part. A groomer really should be handling most of it." I add that last part because I can tell that someone is grooming him regularly. A Goldendoodle's coat would be much longer than this if not.

Celena shakes her head. "Winston snaps at the groomers, too. You have a magic touch, I swear!"

I laugh at her assumption but continue getting all the gunk from, Winston's ears before he gets too restless.

Not all the glory in what I do is life threatening but it's fulfilling. Being that extra hand that owners sometimes need to keep their animals healthy is rewarding. Sure, I've cleaned ears everywhere, but the commonality between every place I've cleaned ears is the love. Choosing to commit to a companion in this way is such a beautiful thing to be a part of. I can love on all the animals I want without the commitment. It's what I can offer and it's more than enough for the animals and their owners. I've always known that this was the job for me.

"Still showing me up right?" Bentley asks from the wall he's leaning on. To the right is a short hallway that leads to the front desk. I can hear Korra chatting happily with Celena about Winston's cleaning.

Tossing my gloves into the trash can in that hall, I turn to face him. "I'd say so. Might have beat my current working time for an ear cleaning." I wave a finger in the air for celebration. It's a little pompous and a whole lot unnecessary. It makes Bentley squint his eyes at me, which tells me I went with a good attack in this situation.

"There is no race for cleaning. It's about doing it thoroughly and effectively. I wouldn't be surprised if Winston is back soon," he retorts.

"I would," I say, frowning at him. "Wishing for a dog to need to come back to the clinic is low, even for you."

He leans down so that his face is only inches from mine. "You're pushing it," he says brusquely.

His face is close enough that I get a whiff of whatever cologne he's wearing or maybe it's the product from his beard. I don't know which, but it instantly brings back memories from that night. That's twice now that I've thought about it today.

Good grief, I need to get a grip on that.

Both of our pagers chime, putting an end to our staring match. When we make it to Korra's desk, she says, "Bean here is up next for you two. She needs a full panel. Dad requested a blood draw for this little lady." *Little lady* couldn't be any more of an inaccurate description for Bean if Korra tried. The Doberman is already a large breed but she is large, even for a Doberman. Her shiny black fur gleams as she seems to know exactly what that means as she circles her owners legs nervously.

"Well you have nothing to fear, Bean." Lee holds a hand out for Bean to sniff and she does so happily. "See. You can trust me. I'm a dog-ter." There are a few chuckles around from everyone except me. "Let's go to room two, okay?" His tone is a little brighter than it would be with me, a fact that irritates me to no end.

He knows how to be somewhat civil to everyone who isn't me. Animals are better than people, but I'm not even a bad person.

"What a great pun," I say with a smile that Alex, Bean's owner recognizes as genuine, but Bentley recognizes as the jab it was intended to be. He deflates only slightly, opening the gate for Alex and Bean to come back to the examination table.

Looking over the folder outside of the room, I see Wayne's notes about possible kidney concerns for Bean.

"She's gonna need a full lab then," Bentley says after reading the information over my shoulder. He looks over to the cabinets that hold the syringes.

"Nose goes," I say, pressing my finger to my nose for him to see and then entering the room. "Hi, Alex. I'm Zadie. You spoke with our vet, Wayne, last about Bean, right?"

"Yes, I want to do whatever we need to for her to feel better."

"Agreed," I nod, writing my notes about Bean's general condition on the chart in my hands. "Before we do anything too elaborate for her, we'll need to get a few samples of blood so that we can test for the possibilities that Wayne was considering. Will that be okay?"

"Of course," Alex pats his dog's head in his lap.

"Great. If you could move her to the table, Bentley will hold her, so that I'm able to get the samples we'll need."

Bentley smiles though it's forced as he preps the syringes.

The doberman jumps onto the table with ease though she seems to understand what is coming next.

Bentley has to use all his strength to hold Bean in place as she wiggles on the table. She isn't resisting *per se*, she's just a large dog who is nervous. Her energy vibrates us both as Bentley does his best to keep her in place for me.

I giggle at his struggle since there is no way I would have been able to restrain her for him to get the samples we needed.

The day goes on like that as the two of us trade off exams and cleanings until Wayne comes in and there is less of our collaboration necessary.

Korra and I take our lunch together, choosing to get sushi since Korra is its biggest fan. While we wait for our food I ask, "How is wedding planning going?"

She immediately goes into the details she's already sorted with Bryce and how excited she is to go look for dresses soon. Though her and her fiancé announced their engagement on Thanksgiving, they set the date for June and I'm stressed just thinking about all the planning she's doing.

"Do you think you'll be able to come for the fitting? I'm not really sure what kind of dress I want to look for so I'll need as many opinions as I can get." Her eyes lose just a hint of their sparkle when she says, "I know it will be hard doing this without Mom, but if I'm surrounded by friends it won't feel like the absence is taking up as much space. You know?"

I lean across the small table we chose to hug her. "Of course," I say. "You don't have to explain anything. Of course I'll be there to help."

That seems to give her a little bit of her shine back in time for the food to come out to us.

When I have given thought to where I would go next after having the opportunity to travel for so long, I dreaded returning to Harmony Hill. All I could remember was how out of place I felt here. I thought that I could find a place that was the perfect fit in any one of the countries I worked in since I graduated college.

Where I found many places I loved and that I'll never forget, there was something missing from all of them. I made friends along the way and saw places that I likely could have made home for longer if I chose to.

But something in me said I needed to come back here.

My purpose in life may not be becoming a bridesmaid though, Korra and Bryce aren't having a wedding party, but little memories like this sure do make me feel warm inside.

Getting the chance to support my friend when she needs it is a special kind of rewarding. It's good to feel needed, but even better to do so for someone who deserves that and more.

Chapter 6

Zadie

"How do you think he's going to react when you tell him that you're moving in?" Kasey asks from where she leans against Korra's sedan. Her fur and leather jacket zipped high and her long, dark hair blowing in the breeze behind her.

Winter is still going strong as the cold afternoon reminds us just how high in elevation we are. It's probably more temperate in Denver than it is here. Seven-thousand feet above sea level guarantees you a cooler climate. February won't let us forget that it is still wintertime.

Looking into the reflection of Korra's rear window beside her *Who's your poppy* bumper sticker, I adjust the ear warmers over my hair so that my curls aren't too smushed. "I don't know, Kasey. It's not like he lives there. I don't even have to tell him."

Yes, I did invite the Thomas family to go ice-skating with me.

Yes, I did intentionally tell Korra to invite her little brother as well.

Yes, I did wear this super cute outfit that turns out to be far more warm than anything else I have in my closet right now with the intention of being both off-limits and incredibly cute.

I'm not above using any tactics in my arsenal to make Bentley feel like the complete ass-hat that he is.

All week he has gone to the next level of being annoying at work. If there's anything that he could make easy for me, he hasn't. And if we have to work together for an animal's treatment, he has made it more than irritating to be in his presence.

Maybe the tool I need is just out of reach or maybe he was the one to move it.

Oh, was I looking for that folder? He already returned it to the filing cabinet.

Everyone is ordering in for lunch? He already submitted the order before I was done with the patient I was working with.

What's the most annoying part of all of this is the fact that he is a completely different person to everyone else at the clinic. I think his Dad getting on his ass about his salty attitude towards other staff members was the heartbreak that he needed. He has been on his very best behavior as of late. As Wayne has decided that he's going to step back even further in doing half days, it leaves us with a lot more time to interact with each other instead of getting what we need done through him.

Bentley saves his worst behavior for me, alone.

I just don't understand what it is that's making him such a pill.

And I'm talking about a horse pill. Like one, the size of your pinky finger.

When I think back to it, all I said was that I was sorry about his breakup. *And he blew off the damn handle!* Or maybe it was about his condo? *Hell, if I know!* It's really not my job to be responsible for whatever his foul mood is. I figure if I can have his family around then maybe he'll act just a little bit less like a jerk and I can get to the bottom of whatever this is today.

Whichever way Wayne decides to move forward with his retirement, we'll be working in the same place. I don't want to work somewhere else. I want to work with my friend. I like where Thomas & Friends is located in town and when I eventually get the keys, it'll be a perfect distance from both my new flat and my family's house.

I don't want to make a major career decision based on one shitty coworker who just needs to get over himself.

"But then it's like you're hiding something," Korra adds unhelpfully. "And this is supposed to be celebrating. I mean we're going for ice cream afterwards."

"That was your idea to do ice cream after ice-skating? You know?" Kasey looks like she's about to say something out-of-pocket. It's clear in her posturing. "I understand that... You know... When you're *getting it good*, it's a little hard to come down to reality, but like... Could we not have gone for... I don't know? Molten lava cake or, hell, I'd take a pie."

Korra giggles, probably messaging her fiancé, when she tells her twin, "You can order whatever you want. But I think it's kind of cute ice-skating, then ice cream it's like an icy celebration. It's on theme. You know I love a good theme..."

She does love a good theme and I don't mind it as much as Kasey. "I am always down for ice cream. Especially if it's got chocolate and nuts in it. And I'm pretty sure this place has both. I think they sell pie, too. Maybe even cake? I think it might be ice cream cake, though."

Kasey lets out a deep sigh that goes up in a white cloud in front of her face. "You two are both out of your minds. If I wasn't actually skating then I wouldn't be opposed to this." She sips from an extra large Thunderbolts mug. "I've got some coffee in my system, I think I can think a little bit more considerately of you two."

Ignoring her sister, Korra puts her phone into her back pocket, looping an arm through mine to continue our previous conversation. "Well, if it helps, Bryce already said that he'd hired a company to help me move things out so we could help move your things in, too. And I'm sure that once we tell Zack and Lee what's going on, they'll also help move things from your parents house into our apartment."

The three of us start walking to where the line for skate rentals are. I can see Zach parking and making his way over to us before he spots Bryce and the two of them greet each other by the time we get a spot in line.

“The Zach part I can completely understand. But I have a really hard time believing that *Bent* is going to do anything to help me in any way." Throwing my hands in the air, I add, "You see how he is at work.”

Speak of the devil himself, the roar of his engine interrupts whatever Korra was going to say before Bentley parks his truck.

Why did I invite him again?

Oh, right—To find out how to remove that stick...

I purse my lips to keep from saying what I’m thinking aloud as I glare at the back of his head when he talks to the other men coming over to join us.

“You know the tension between you two is so thick. I would think that there’s something more going on there... And from past experience, I have to say that I’m never wrong about these things...”

The laugh that comes tumbling out of my body is more of a honk than anything else. I don’t know if it sounds so absurd because I am guilty of what Kasey is implying or because I am nervous that she has actually clocked what has happened between Bentley and I. “Don’t be ridiculous! He is just an ass.”

Korra looks at me for a few more moments before adding to her sister's speculation. “I think Kasey's got a point. There’s something else there. I’ve never seen him be this active about being rude to anyone. I mean, he’s not a particularly pleasant person to be around when he’s upset. But it’s not really been like this with anyone. You’re the only one that really makes him go like super ballistic butthole.”

“Super ballistic butthole... You know I really like that, Korra. I think I’m gonna have to use it.”

“I don’t think you’re hurting for any insults.” Kasey looks at her sister and then back to me. “But I do think that something else is going on here and that honking-ass laugh you let out earlier makes me feel like something else is going on. It’s cold, but it’s not that cold—your cheeks are red hot.”

“They are not,” I screech, pressing a mitten-covered palm to my face. “I’m just getting chilly because we’ve been standing over here for a while.”

Kasey’s lips twist to the side. “Yea and my hair actually grows from my head the same fire-engine red that yours does.”

"I've been meaning to tell you that I love the red highlights. I think it really does suit your skin tone."

"Nice deflection," she says in a droll tone that belies her compliment. "You're almost as good as Korra was when her and Bryce were becoming a thing. Remember when they were *just friends* and now all of a sudden they're getting married in like... in June! I'm never wrong."

"Okay, I'm not even a part of the Thomas family. So the inquisition has got to stop. I said there's nothing going on and there's not. He's just a jerk to me. I have to work with him—we're not friends. He's pissed that I'm an actual competition for a spot he thought he was guaranteed to have. If it were anyone else, he would probably still be the same jerk to them. I just happen to be the cutest thing in the office." Korra makes an exaggerated cough. "I mean that's not related to him. Obviously," I correct for Korra's benefit.

"Whatever you say, girl," Kasey says, not sounding convinced at all.

It is whatever I say, I say to myself in my head.

Chapter 7

Lee

"You could maybe try to *not* scowl..." Korra says as I cross my arms to keep a little warmer out here.

Snow is piled high around the edge of a slick white ice rink surface. Going skating outdoors used to be one of my favorite things to do in the wintertime. I don't go as often as I used to when I was younger, but my sister insisted that we all go since it's not as busy now that winter is almost over. There's likely only a week or two left before they close this rink down for the season. Spring isn't that far off, but February did not get the memo. It's still freezing out.

I rub my hands against an instant hand warmer pack in my pocket to get some feeling in them. I've been standing in line with my family all chattering around me for the past twenty-five minutes.

"There are children around and I would hate for you to scare them all off," Korra continues.

My eyebrows only bunch tighter when I respond, "You know I could try not scowling..." I tilt my head toward the left, "or you could try not inviting Zadie everywhere that the family goes."

The woman in question simply adjusts her fuzzy ear-warming headband so that it's tighter over her ears. She's wearing a fuzzy pink sweater that has these ridiculous fuzzy pink cuffs. The cuffs match her ear warmer so maybe they aren't actually attached to this humongous sweater. In white tights and a frilly white skirt that flounces over her generous hips, I can't imagine that this outfit is the warmest that she could manage for skating on ice. Not even the fuzzy pink leg warmers over her pink suede boots could make up for the fact that she's not wearing pants.

Korra only laughs as she snuggles tighter to her fiancé. "Zadie actually made these plans and invited us to come with. Maybe you should be a little more grateful that your name was mentioned at all." Her tone is bright when she says the words, though they shock the hell out of me.

Why would she invite me?

The last week has been us at each other's throats. And it's not just me. Zadie is the type to deliver a blow with a smile and her little pigtail braids. No one understands how absolutely devious she can be. I'm finding out first hand that I don't enjoy being on the receiving end of her cunning.

"Yea, *Bent*. You should be a little more grateful," Zadie says as we finally move forward in line. The sun is setting a little later with Spring approaching, but it's too dark for my liking at this point in the day. A gust of wind blows through the line sending little chips of snow and ice from the surrounding trees our way.

Looking her figure up and down as she stands tall in the chilly air, I note, "That's a lot of big talk coming from someone who came skating with no pants on."

"Why are you so worried about whether or not I'm wearing pants?" She asks with a smirk. "Layering is essential. If you must know, these are fur-lined tights, so they're much better than a pair of jeans." She points towards my own pants and how I am clearly more cold than she is. I pop the collar to my coat to shield my neck from the cold air a little more.

Kasey cackles, "He is freezing. You can totally tell. Little cold there, Lee?"

"Ah ah ah. No one is fighting today. Everyone is going to put on a smiling face and enjoy quality time with one another." Zach intervenes, though I didn't ask for his help. I glare at the back of his head. He's never beating the allegations about him being a goodie-two-shoes. No one is around for him to impress and he's still sticking to his peace-keeper tendencies. *Figures.*

"That is a good rule. I wish I had said that first," Korra says, taking her friend by the arm as her and Bryce are next in line.

It's our turn to rent skates and everyone tells the few attendants their shoe sizes, so that we can finally get onto the ice.

"Should I be surprised that you actually know how to ice skate?" Zadie says, standing over me as I'm still lacing up my rentals. Her legs look even longer than usual while I'm kneeling in front of her. With her hands on her hips, she takes notice of the imbalance of our power in this way. The spark of it registers in her light eyes.

"I think it's fair to say that you thinking I'm skilled at anything is shocking. Seems to be a default setting for you." As frustrating as it is, she wouldn't be wrong that she is better at most things than I am.

In this particular case, I either had to learn how to ice skate or be humiliated by shuffling along the edge of the rink growing up while my siblings took to the ice well. My Mom always took us to do this together, but I hadn't made time to do it for a while.

It was time with her that I had missed. Now, I wish I hadn't put it off. I never knew that I wouldn't get another chance to skate with her, carefree in the fresh winter air.

Bryce, Zach, and I are the last on the ice, while Korra, Kasey, and Zadie are already making their way towards the other side. I'm a little shaky at first, but after a short adjustment period I get my bearings and the ladies lap us.

The even numbers meant that as soon as we all got together again, everyone sort of paired up. The two love birds skate arm in arm around the rink as they talk about who-knows-what mushy shit. *Likely their upcoming wedding.* Zach and Kasey are also skating and talking with each other, which leaves me and Zadie to our own devices.

At first there is only the sound of generic pop music that plays from the speakers in the rink between us. I'm lucky that with the activity, I've started to warm up more and can relax if it's only the smallest bit.

The music changes to a song that I'm surprised to hear since Colorado, and Harmony Hill, is not well-known for its diversity in music. But I recognize it well since I'm a fan of the band. It doesn't escape my notice that Zadie is singing along to the music too as we glide along the ice.

"You know this group?"

Her head swivels to face me with an eyebrow raised. "You know PFP? Did I already hit my head on the ice or something?"

"Huh?" I ask, unsure of what she's trying to say.

She rubs at her temple for effect. "I must be concussed or something. You like K-Pop? Since when?"

I shrug because it's not been very long. When only sad thoughts are associated with the music I've known, I started looking for music that had no attached memories of Mom. In the past few months, it's taken me to some places I've not been before. I can't say that I like the genre as a whole, but I have heard a few groups that are entertaining and dare I say it, fun. It's interesting to listen to and creative. "I like good music. These guys make some good music."

"Hmm," is all she says for a while.

Korra laughs at something just in front of us that has Bryce laughing in turn. Yea, as expected, these two are doing what they do best–be in their own little world.

Zadie continues her thought saying, "You won't believe how good they sound live too. All while dancing? It's truly an experience."

Jealously spikes as I consider how much fun a concert put on by this group would be. "You've seen PFP live? When?"

She nods, looking proud of herself. "When I lived in Korea. I got pictures." She searches in her sweater's pocket for her phone, I'm guessing. Should have known that she would have something else to brag about.

While she's distracted, a kid loses control of some sort of spin he's doing on the ice and careens towards us. On instinct, I grab Zadie by the waist to move her out of the way of the oncoming collision. Somehow maneuvering us to only be briefly swiped by the kid who eventually lands on his butt. He apologizes profusely, but I just say, "It's okay, little man. You just need a little more work."

Instead of sticking around for more of his apologies, I keep moving us along. Zadie remains pointedly quiet and it's not until I look down that I notice why. *My hand is still on her waist*. It's a firm hold as I guide us along the curved side of the rink.

She's soft and warm in my grip. The sweater is pleasant under my fingers, but it's really her shape that pleases me. I know very well how good she feels in my hold like this and that's a problem for me.

"Feel free to release me at any point..." Zadie says when I fail to let go of her sides.

I drop my hands immediately as if she's burned me. In some way as she has. I'm not thirsting after her or trying to cop a feel.

I want the opposite.

This was an accident.

What I want is to forget the fact that her and I know each other's bodies intimately.

I know that men get a bad reputation for collecting beautiful women as trophies to use and discard. But I've never been a man who has ever felt that women were a commodity to collect. I've been lucky enough to date a few beautiful women. Malaya and everything that happened there is not exactly an ideal circumstance to reminisce on. But if I allow myself to not feel guilty about it, I would reminisce about being with Zadie. And that's what makes this all fucked up.

"Hey look, they've got the stand open now," Zadie says as she points to the well lit food stand next to the skate rental booth. We're on the straight side of the rink now where people can enter at their own pace. Unwilling to dodge more unsteady skaters, I push further to the center and Zadie keeps up with me unaware of her acquiescence to follow.

There's a giggle in her voice as she says, "And what do you know? They're even serving cider." Her eyebrows raise high on her forehead. She knows exactly what the thought of cider would make me recall. What's more interesting is that *she's trying* to make me recall it.

But two can play that game.

"Well, it's funny that you bring that up..." I start and she doesn't correct me, simply waiting for where I'm going with my statement. "You seem to think a lot about how I could make you feel the way you did. Was it the cider that had you moaning or was it me?"

I keep a straight face to ensure she will feel even more flustered by recalling the night that she clearly hasn't forgotten.

Even in the cool winter air Zadie's cheeks and nose were only mildly reddened. But now they bloom a vibrant shade as she gives me a vivid display of the memories she's recalling.

"I believe that you believe that," Zadie says before skiing ahead of me.

I only have a view of her curls and the swish of her hips when I say, "Pink looks good on you, but I think green and red are still my favorite."

She whips around, curls flying in turn. That night I remember the flush of her golden brown skin in contrast with the green lingerie that she wore. I told her as much. It might not have been intentional to say that night, but I would never forget how it made her blush even harder. *I can't forget it actually.* It brings a smile to my lips that I can't begin to hide as her eyes sear me.

I know there's a retort on her lips and I'd be eager to hear what she has to say in return, but my sister and Bryce end up lapping us and skating behind where we are. "Hey, we're gonna stop to get some snacks. I think this is the same stand that had the apple cider donuts Bryce and I had at the Fall Extravaganza last year. They were so good!" Her ring glints in the bright lights as she holds her fiancé closer. "Even if it's not them, I still want to get some. Warm donuts and cider while it's freezing outside sounds like the best kind of treat."

Zadie's eyes narrow on me. With her back to my sister, Korra can't see the expression that her friend is giving me.

"Sure," I agree as the two of them skate off to catch Kasey and Zach too.

The six of us find a spot to eat our sweets and warm our hands with our drinks. I pointedly ordered a hot coffee instead of a cider, though the way Zadie smiles as she enjoys hers and talks with Korra and Kasey makes me wish that I had gone for something sweeter than a black coffee.

When she talks to my sisters, her personality is so different from how she interacts with me. You might even say she's nice.

I'm sure she is nice. She has no reason not to be nice to my sisters. They love her. If I hadn't known any better, I'd say that this was a family outing like any other.

Hell, I had.

She's acting like she's already a part of this family.

She is not my sister though.

She will never be.

It's been years since I've had to worry about her being around because she had been traveling and, now, I can't escape her.

Now, I'm having to process this person in front of me as something other than my work nemesis.

Nemesis feels exaggerated and over the top. *This isn't a comic book.* But I do think that there is an underlying maliciousness to how thoroughly she is besting me at work. *I'm not incompetent.* I'm not even bad at my job. I just have a lot of shit on my mind.

Zach and Bryce are talking about something I have completely lost track of as I watch my sisters' friend laugh her throaty laugh with them.

I wonder if she's told them about that night.

Do I think that she would share those details with my sister? I don't know how much of her sex life she shares with anyone. With the whole boho-have-no-home-floating-on-the-wind-like-a-leaf type of attitude she has I would think that no topic is off-limits. But seeing as how neither of my sisters have asked me anything about it... seems she's keeping this particular interaction close to the chest unless it's to gloat to me.

Is she embarrassed by what we did?

Does she not want people to know that we were together?

God, that is a stupid line of thinking.

I don't want people to know that it happened.

I'm not feeling any type of way about the fact that my sisters don't know that I hooked up with their friend.

Chapter 8

Zadie

Just because I invited him here doesn't mean anything.

Obviously.

My goal in him coming to this rink with everyone was very simple. And I've managed to, not only, get a little bit caught up with his hands on my waist earlier and then, now as he sits talking with his brother and soon to be brother-in-law, I find myself a little bit worried about even broaching the subject.

That's so unlike me.

Also, it's Bentley.

What do I have to be worried about?

I'm sure there is all sorts of vitriol that he could spout off about. I mean, he had a problem with my cute little pink outfit! Which is cute and there's no reason to be upset about it considering it's not affecting him in any way...

I smirk internally, just thinking... I guess it sort of is.

He is absolutely enraptured with this outfit, considering he's found more than one reason to touch me. I'm not playing fair and I don't have to.

This is a celebration of my new flat. We're celebrating and I'm not going to let anything Bentley has to say about my choices affect that.

When everybody's done with their treats and back on the ice for one last skate around the rink, I figure it's the best time to break the news since everyone still partnered up in the way that they originally were.

My brain said to tell him the news, unfortunately my eyes had different plans. I don't know why it's standing out to me now, but I need to comment on it. "I see you're really leaning into this whole beard thing..."

I don't hate the beard. Honestly, it's a pretty good look on him.

When I first started working at Thomas & Friends, it was just a bit of scruff like he had forgotten to shave for a few days. Sometimes, he'd actually line it up, but it seems like he's leaning further and further away from the razor.

The combination of him in glasses and a beard is not *unpleasant*. It actually looks better on him than, I think, anyone else. I knew that he needed glasses, but I never really saw him wear them until I moved back to town.

It's pretty cute to see him get frustrated when they slide down his nose. Gotta admit I really just like seeing him be frustrated. Doesn't matter what the cause is. For such an irritating person, seeing him be irritated and not by my hand is pretty great.

Bentley cuts into my memories of his frustrated face, when he says, "Yea, well, it's cold out. And the beard keeps me just a little bit warmer."

"I see..."

Why is it so hard to just tell him?

Ugh. Just let him know that I'm moving in with his sister, Z.

I know he'll have an issue with it. And there's no way he won't find out eventually. It's just the right thing to tell him outright.

Right?

Gliding along the ice, I allow myself to fall behind him. To the back of his head, I say, "So I've kind of got some news that you would be interested to know."

He turns, the spin surprisingly graceful, to face me and skate backward. "You've got news?" There is a flutter in my stomach. Maybe this would have been easier to say skating beside him. His skating backward is impressive and unexpected. I could prolong this conversation further by asking him about it, though it won't serve me in any way.

Instead, I say."Yes..." Just pull up your big girl panties and come out with Zadie! "I'm moving in with Kasey after Korra moves out of their flat to her new house."

He simply looks at me for a few moments. The lightness of his eyes are hard to read, though the eyebrows are a dead giveaway. There's a hard set in the line of his lips.

Maybe I didn't say it loud enough?

No, he definitely heard me.

I fiddle with one of my curls while I give him time to, *hopefully*, reply. Being on sharp ice knives as people are hurrying around us is not a good place to be distracted, so I hope that whatever it is he's thinking about–he gets control of it soon.

"So there is just no getting rid of you?" He asks with only confusion on his face now.

And there we go.

His rudeness knows no bounds.

"What is your problem? The appropriate response is, 'Great' or better yet saying nothing at all."

He shakes his head, still skating backward, "Why do you insist on getting closer to my family? I'm sure there are other places you could live in this town."

"B*ent*, I'm doing your sisters a huge favor. Specifically Kasey. It would be difficult for her to find a roommate with this short notice. Not to mention, my best friend Korra, shouldn't have to worry about her twin stressing when she just got a beautiful new home with her fiancé. Don't you want her to be happy?"

He stops abruptly in front of me. I don't have the wherewithal to swerve him in time. His hands land on my waist again, holding me only an inch or two from his body. I'm keenly aware of the heat coming off him.

Looking up into his eyes, the intensity there is enough to pause my accusations. I want to say more but the complexity of his gaze arrests me.

Why did my words elicit this reaction?

On the tip of my tongue is, "*What's wrong*?" I don't say it, but I want to know why. I didn't say anything particularly spicy. Or mean...

"Bentley–"

"When are you moving in?" He asks. I'm not sure why exactly I expected him to expand on this expression, this intensity, but he isn't going to. That much is clear.

Stop, Zadie. It's not your problem.

You don't care.

But I do care about his hands still on me. The warmth in stark contrast to the ice in his eyes.

"Tomorrow," I say in a low tone though, it's loud enough to be heard over the chatter and ambient slicing of ice around us.

He rolls his eyes, finally releasing me to skate beside me again. "Of course. There is never any time for me to recover from you, is there?"

He asked the question, but skates ahead hard and fast.

I don't try to catch up with him, choosing to recover from the tangle of emotions I feel about this.

There is no way I was going to figure out why he can't stand me. I won't even get to ask him to come for ice cream later so that I can get to the bottom of it.

Korra eventually catches up to me at my slower pace and links one of her arms with mine. "Lee said he had to go do something. More ice cream for us right?"

"Right," I say with a smile in place that I don't feel.

Chapter 9

Lee

"See, this is exactly what I'm talking about," I huff from behind a large moving box in my hands. "Of all the places she could live in town, she picks my sisters' flat."

The flat in question almost looks foreign without the plethora of planters and greenery that normally covers most of the open space. The only thing that remains of Korra's plant addiction is a single Ivy by Kasey's door that I can see from the entryway. It's surprising how much larger the flat looks without the leaves everywhere.

"Will you give it a rest already? You act like she forced her way in here. She's actually helping us out quite a bit, considering the fact that I was the one who suggested that she take my half of the rent," Korra says. I already know that because Zadie said the same. *It doesn't matter who is saying it.* I still can't get away from this woman and the universe is working its very hardest to push us into the same arena.

Setting the box down, I ask, "Did you even try to find someone else to fill the space?"

"Why in the hell would she do that, *Broken*?" Zadie comes from around the corner with both of her arms full of extra-large nylon tote bags that appear to have nothing but spandex outfits in them.

I assume it's her entire wardrobe of yoga clothing. I've only caught sight of her in her workout clothes on the weekends. Occasionally, I'll see one of these brightly colored outfits hanging from her massive shoulder bag. To believe that they fill up two bags that big is too much for my brain right now.

She pushes her way beside me to throw them into what was once my sister's room. A hint of her spiced apple scent wafts out behind her. *Must everything remind me of that night?*

Damn.

"You know you could've just said you were busy instead of coming today?" Kasey says, carrying two smaller boxes into the house. "If you're not going to play well with my new roommate, then I suggest that you find somewhere else to play."

"You could've asked Zack to do this," I grumble.

Kasey doesn't get a chance to respond because Zadie is back in the living room to sass me. "Yes, we did ask Zack before we asked you. Are you hard of hearing or what? No one wanted your grumpy ass here, but a strong back is a strong back. And since we're in our thirties, there's not a lot of strong backs to call on."

"You could've hired a moving service like you did to get all of Korra's things out of here and into their new house."

"Yea, the rest of us aren't making lawyer kind of money so we're gonna rely on the friends and family discount A.K.A. free labor because we're blood relatives," Korra says before leaving Kasey and I in the living room alone to get more things from Zadie's obnoxious yellow SUV.

"Why are you being such an annoying pest? When we were teenagers, it kind of made sense because all teenagers are really... the worst. But you're a grown man. So I don't really understand why it is that you can't just give her a break. Whatever it is that you two had going on just squash it. You're adults. People go after the same job all the time. It doesn't have to be this contentious. Besides, it seems completely one-sided considering the fact that she hasn't done anything." I open my mouth but Kasey holds a finger up. "She actually asked us to not ask you. To which, I promptly told her that I would be asking you twice as much now. What is your problem?"

I decide against saying that *she vowed to be the bane of my existence.* Korra returns with another bag of Zadie's. Instead of returning to the SUV, she goes to join her twin. My reasoning would do no good in a room full of women who all think that I'm in the wrong anyway.

I wish that I could let it go.

And I probably would have if I were sane.

But the thing is that I'm not.

She has driven me past sanity.

In a place where I normally would find my small moments of joy and happiness around working with animals, which is something I've wanted to do my entire life, Zadie has made it unbelievably stressful. *Her mere presence is a threat to me.* I'm second-guessing myself at every turn. I'm constantly doing more work than I should just to have my name on more completed paperwork or exams.

It's exhausting and aggravating.

Zadie comes into the room, standing beside my sisters. "I'm letting you off the hook, *Broken.* Feel free to exit from the front door. There are three strong women here and even if your sisters weren't here, I'd be able to do it. I moved my shit around for years by myself from country to country. It would be no different just moving twenty minutes from my parents house to here."

"Yes, yes. I get it." Narrowing my eyes, I continue, "You're strong, you *don't need no man* and I'm here proving that all men are the worst. Have I got that right?"

All three women nod, but Zadie says, "Seems about right to me. I even offered to provide dinner and drinks later on. I'm rescinding that invitation from your way."

Rolling my eyes, "Again, I ask, why is Zach not here?"

"Zach is starting his three-day shift tonight. We're not gonna let him wear himself out to help Zadie move when we have a perfectly capable, using that word generously in this case, person to help out." Kasey takes a seat on the edge of the couch to sip from her football cup. "It's not like Zadie even has that much since she hasn't been living here in years."

"Exactly. I don't–"

Her argument dies mid sentence as her phone rings in the back pocket of the jeans she's wearing. She pulls out the phone, which is ringing obnoxiously. I didn't even know that people left their ringer on anymore.

Is she not a millennial?

I know my phone lives on silent.

But her and I are obviously very different people.

She checks who's calling for only a moment before picking up. "Hi, Wayne. How are you doing?"

My dad's calling her?

"Oh yea, I've got pretty much everyone here. They shouldn't be too long if you need them." She looks me up and down while she listens to whatever it is my Dad is saying on the other line.

"What's he saying?" I mouth to her, but she just holds up a finger as she continues to listen to what he said.

Why is he calling her instead of me? If it's something that's important, does he have to talk to her about it on a Sunday? It could wait until next week surely.

"Oh, I'd love to be a part of it," she says as she looks me dead in the eye. There's an intensity in her gaze when she says the next words. "I think it'd be fair if both Bentley and I were able to show up for this event."

She nods, though he can't see her. "Really let them know that the Thomas & Friends clinic is a reliable member of this community. Two sets of hands are always better than one," she laughs though it sounds polite instead of genuine.

"A community partner with what," I whisper. She just holds her finger up again as my Dad is saying something in response to her volunteering my time.

"Oh, well, I think he's around here somewhere I'll be sure to let him know. Or you can give him a call if you'd like." I can hear my dad's laugh on the other side of the line though she still has the phone pressed to her ear. "I don't blame you. Mmmhmm, I'll let him know."

She ends the call and I'm still wondering what it is she's talking about.

When she doesn't immediately begin telling me what they talked about I ask, "So are you gonna tell me what it is you volunteered me for or should I just guess?"

Zadie is smug when she says, "I would love nothing more than to let you know what we will be working on together." She takes a seat beside Kasey but instead of perching on the edge, she sprawls backward, her arms stretching across the back. She's stalling and setting my nerves on edge the more time she takes to just tell me. I grind my teeth waiting for her to which Kasey only chuckles at.

Finally Zadie says, "So, the Brenfords are still having a lot of issues, who knows what that's about, but they are backing out of being the main sponsor for the adoption drive that normally Wayne is just overseeing the medical care for. Now we're going to be doing, not only the medical care, but will be facilitating the event as well!" Her smile grows. "Doesn't that sound like fun? A spring pet adoption drive held by Thomas & Friends. Especially with their new vet being able to greet them as a lifelong partner in their new pets' care."

"And let me guess you volunteered me to work the drive?" I ask as I cross my arms over my chest. I would not be surprised if she had me in the most guest-facing role available so that she could be working as the actual vet, examining all of the pets.

In past years, the adoption centers from different local counties would come together for a big event held by the Brenford family. My Dad was medical staff, so he would oversee any spaying, neutering, vaccines, etc. to get the pets ready for adoptions before the event actually commenced. I had helped him with the project, but my name was never anywhere near it. And I definitely wasn't talking to any of the people who were going to adopt.

"Of course I did," she coos, giddy to share what she's done. "You're so good with the patients. And on top of that, it'll give him a really clear idea of who the next vet should be. I mean, after all, may the best woman win." Zadie gives Kasey a shoulder bump. "And she will."

She's so puffed up and I hate it. "This is not an end to this competition between us. There's still just as much chance for me to end up with that role as you."

"I wouldn't be so sure about that. Your Dad mentioned that he is looking forward to doing a bit of traveling himself. And even asked for some recommendations on places he should go–as I am an expert..." Self satisfied and more than willing to dangle any of her accomplishments in front of my face, she says, "Can't imagine that he could be the veterinarian in the office while he is out of the country for several months."

He did not say that.

He definitely didn't say anything about that to me. "There's no way that he said that in the time that you were on the phone just now."

"Oh no, it wasn't while we were on the phone just now. We were talking about it in the office last week. *On your off day.* I had just brought up how I was able to see so many things and really maximize my time when traveling. He was intrigued, so we got to talking. And what do you know? He was looking for travel within the next three months. I assume he'd want to get his affairs in order before he left town, don't you?"

I take the few steps to get into her space, uncaring that my sisters are still here. "There's no way that he would be leaving town without telling Korra about it at least. You're bluffing. No, not even a bluff. This is a full lie and I don't understand why you're doing it."

Korra makes a sound, but Kasey puts a hand on her arm. "Zadie's on a roll," she murmurs to her twin, always willing to be nosy in other people's business.

"Now, now, *Broken*. Korra already knows. We talked about it over lunch. He'll be here for the wedding, of course, but is thinking of leaving right after. There is no need for me to lie. I'm just stating facts. It's not looking too good for you." She taps her wrist where a watch should be, but isn't. "The clock is running out and so far, I'm in the lead. Think I'm actually about to lap you, dearie."

"Nothing has been decided," I say, backing away from her. Grabbing my coat, I walk toward the hallway to leave. "I've still got a dog in this fight. The adoption drive is only going to exhaust you and give me a greater advantage."

"Sure thing," she says, still relaxing on the couch.

I leave the flat, irritated and uncertain. With every mind to call my Dad and confirm all that Zadie has said. But I don't.

If I call him now, then there would be no end to the questions I have for him.

Zadie got what she wanted. She won this round.

Just like she always seems to.

Chapter 10

Zadie

"I love what you're doing for this holiday. Though I'm not the biggest Valentine's Day fan–I do love all the decorations." And I did love all of them. If anybody was a fan of a theme, it was Korra.

The office looked like Valentine's Day had exploded all over it. She had even bought a bunch of really cute headbands and little heart clips for any of the patients that were coming in. As I walked Sammy, the little Chihuahua, out to her owner, Korra was happy to give her the heart ears headband that she wore proudly after an amazing exam with me and Wayne.

I wish I could say that everyone in the office was feeling the love... But there was one grumpy man in particular who was not at all feeling, especially, affectionate.

Well, not towards me. Because Princess, the wire-haired pup, in his arms was getting many, many kisses. So much so that her owner had to pull her off of him. He brushed some of the kisses from his cheek and said, "What can I say? I guess it's just puppy love?"

Blech.

To top everything off, he had some sort of pun to go along with it.

Bentley just could not help himself. Princess was now having a little heart clipped onto her fur on the top of her head. And of course, Jack, who was holding her, laughed along with the pun.

I made quick work of handing my paperwork to Korra, so I could get back to the employee break room. The sooner I did not have to show my displeasure with how *pleasant* he was with everyone else here, the better.

Checking my phone after washing my hands, I scrolled through notifications but none of them were from a Valentine.

I'd come back home looking for stability and I had found a great job right away. My luck should be on the higher end of the spectrum.

I wasn't expecting to just walk into Harmony Hill and have a ring on my finger or anything, but I haven't been on one date since I've gotten back into town.

And I'm not counting the Christmas fiasco with Bentley as anything other than a drunken lapse in judgement. Actually, I wasn't counting it as anything at all!

I'm still actively pushing that thought from my mind. He was never a viable option though my mind unhelpfully brought the idea up.

Bentley has shown me that the only thing that he was interested in was my body, for the very brief moment that he was very highly intoxicated on the cider that he openly mocked and then drank the whole gallon of...

Heavy, annoyed sigh.

A mistake I don't have to make twice. Right?

I mean... the dating apps aren't the best place to do that, but I had to start somewhere.

I wanted to get through as many of the *are you new in town?* interactions as possible, so I could find somebody who really was looking for a partner.

Not just a hook up.

So far, no such luck.

I'm not letting it affect me and my confidence though. Valentine's Day is still going on. I have plans to go to the bar tonight and just mingle. I'm sure there are plenty of other single people in Harmony Hill that would love my company.

The prospects are not too bad. There seems to be about the same number of men as women in this club. I am happy to see that.

Korra recommended that I come here since she had a great time on her birthday last year. The DJ has a pretty good mix of popular songs and country that I'm familiar with. It's a vibe with just enough room that people can dance comfortably on the dance floor and still get to the bar. It has two floors. The bottom floor seems to be mostly dancing and the single bar on the back wall. There are a set of open stairs that lead to a second floor. The top floor is partially open, so I'm sure when the weather is nice it is even nicer. But in winter, they have most of it closed off. It is clearly for lounging. Many of the tables and booths are occupied, but it is less busy than the main floor. Looks like where I want to start since I came here alone.

Kasey was my first invite but she said she doesn't prescribe to *Valentine's Day clubbing*, so she's going to be at the flat with a guy she's been seeing. I am not allowed to tell Korra or any of her siblings about it since she's seeing him in secret. Could not tell you what that is about, but I know I don't want to be at the flat for whatever she has planned with him.

I sip my drink and find a seat at the opposite end of the bar which, thankfully. I'm able to do easily.

Now that I've got my drink it's time to figure out if anybody in this place is even worth talking to.

Ask and you shall receive.

The lighting is not that great here. Every now and again there's a spotlight that goes around in different colors. There is someone, but I can't quite make out their face in the dim lighting of the club. There is something about their energy though. I can feel the butterflies in my tummy already.

Cutting through the crowd, I see him making purposeful steps towards the upper level that I'm on. He climbs the steps and I have to admire that he has a great ass. It's tight, but not too big. Thick thighs down to black leather boots that go well with this whole leather jacket situation he's got going.

Very nice.

I sit up a little taller and adjust my sweater to show a little more of my shoulder.

By the time he reaches the top steps, he's already headed over to the bar that I'm sitting at.

Oh, maybe my luck has changed.

The music thumps happily and I'm bobbing along to a song I don't really recognize, but the beat is catchy.

I was bobbing until I realized that my luck has definitely not changed.

To my horror, as he gets closer to where I'm sitting, I can actually see the features of his face.

Every positive thing I said about this mystery man, I take back!

The sneer is already on my face as I feel deceived—no, tricked—by this demon-in-disguise of low lighting. "What are you doing here?" I look at him from head to toe. He's wearing a slim cut top and jeans. His leather jacket still over his shoulders with the hint of red down the sleeve.

Dammit.

Why does he look so good?

And did he line up his beard?

Dammit, he had a haircut.

Bentley looks around me, like he's on high alert for thieves or something before he answers, "I'm here to make sure that you don't do anything foolish."

"Me?" I place an indignant hand on my chest. "*To make sure I'm not doing anything foolish…?* Isn't it foolish that you came here in the first place? Aren't you busy brooding and hating everyone?"

He tilts his head to the side, sniffing hard. "I don't hate everyone."

And he looks like he really believes that—which is absurd.

"Oh, that's right. You just hate me. For no reason what-so-freaking-ever." Standing from my bar stool, I say, "If you don't mind, I'm trying to look single and you standing here is making it look like we're having some sort of a couple spat. *Which we aren't*," I say quickly. "'Cause I'm single. And no one invited you here. I learned my lesson in trying to invite you to do things already. I refuse to do that anymore."

He considers me for a moment but settles on, "Yea, well, it's Valentine's Day. Everybody knows that dudes are exceptionally horny at this time. Since my sisters and brother all have things that they're doing I am the only one here that is gonna be able to keep you safe."

"Keep me safe? What is this? I'm in *Harmony Hill*. There's no place safer than a small town like this one." I feel as pompous as I sound when I remind him, "And if you haven't forgotten, I've been all over the world, *basically*, and I have never had any issues with keeping myself safe in the past."

His eyes narrow, but he doesn't move out of my way so that I can walk away from him. I'm blocked in by his big body and I know he's doing it on purpose. "Be that as it may, I'm here. So, just do what you're doing and I'm gonna be around."

I huff.

He's not serious right now. "Can you *being around*, be like, in the parking lot? No one is going to come over here and talk to me when you're standing here like a hulking bodyguard."

Case in point, a couple gets up from the bar beside me and now there is an open spot. Bentley takes the stool, putting a hand on the back of mine so that I'm still not able to leave. "No, I'm actually good right here."

"Just wait outside, Bent."

"Is that where you're going to be?"

Finishing the remnants of my drink, I slide it to the back of the bar, "Nah, it's cold as hell outside. We know I don't like to be cold."

He tuts. "Well coming to Colorado, specifically to the actual hills of Colorado, seems like a really bad choice for you then, huh?" I scowl at him before the bartender comes over to ask if I want another drink. To which I agree whole heartedly. I need another to deal with this turn of events.

"Look, I am pretty sure that you won't have any issue in picking up some dude. He'll only talk to you for about..." He tilts his head from side to side, thinking before he decides on, "this weekend and move on. So if you could hurry that up, then we both will be able to leave as soon as possible."

My drink arrives and I sip from it, correcting, "You could leave right now. There is nothing stopping you from walking right out the door. Or better yet while you're here, you could pick up some unsuspecting girl who thinks that you are *actually charming*. You've got this tight biker situation going on. Ladies like that."

"Tight biker..." He tests the words in his mouth like I'm not speaking English. Which is another absurd thing that he's doing. He is literally wearing a motorcycle jacket. I'm sure he rode his bike here. So what is there to get?

"Yeah, you got this tight ass shirt on and tight ass jeans and this," my finger circles the air in front of me, encompassing his person, "jacket, which is doing too much for my sake."

He raises an eyebrow over the rim of his glasses. "Did you check out my ass?"

I splutter and hack, "No!"

Backtracking is my best option right now because obviously I did. Unfortunately, it was before I fully recognized him.

It's not my fault.

He has a nice ass in these jeans.

The man is clearly working out. I can't say it's hurting his appeal with me–unfortunately.

I had made the mistake in thinking that I was going to be going home with someone else tonight.

I hadn't planned on being sober for the sole benefit of being able to drive home.

Since no one gets under my skin quite like Bentley, I definitely drank too much. And there is not a single other prospect that I have. He never went anywhere else but my side in the bar. I can walk but there is no way I'll get behind the wheel.

But he's sober.

Dammit.

I should just pay for a ride share, but I know I'll be waiting here for at least another thirty minutes considering there aren't that many ride shares in this town.

I really don't wanna ask him

I feel like he's going to be a complete ass about it.

Just pull up your big girl panties. It's better to know if you need to order a ride here now.

I could likely walk home faster than I could get a ride share and I really don't want to because it's so cold...

Ugh.

"Could you give me a ride home?" I ask matter of factly. No emotion. It's just a question.

I have options, sort of.

As we stand under the awning in front of the club entrance, he looks down at me. "Home? To my sister's flat? I don't know..."

Throwing my hands up in the air, I exclaim, "Oh, come on, Bent! I'd be able to have someone else take me home if you hadn't come here and put your bad vibes all around me. So really it's your fault that I'm not able to leave without you."

He rubs his hands together to warm them. "Actually it's the four or five drinks that you had while you scowled at me which is why you can't leave without me."

I was going to kick him.

I was going to kick him and I was going to walk my ass home in the cold.

"Fine. Have it your way," I say, holding a pretend phone up to my ear.

Was it petty?

Yes.

Did my drunken brain have any idea how petulant it was?

No.

"I'm just going to call Korra and let her know that you left me stranded at this club because you were too busy trying to be whatever the hell this was and ruined their first Valentine's Day as fiancés." I purse my lips and shake my head. "They'll never forgive you."

He rolls his eyes and tilts his head towards the lot. "You know which bike's mine."

It's as if he is incapable of just being a chill human being.

Everything he does is irritating as hell.

Marching over to the red one parked in the front with his motorcycle parking privilege, I stand beside it, trying to secure the strap to my purse.

He takes it from me to put in the saddle bag, which I didn't realize could hold my purse, without a word.

I get on the back of his bike and though the seat is large enough to accommodate us both. I still feel a little self-conscious as I'm right on the back edge. He sits in front of me and gives me zero extra space. I know there's not much room with my ass, but I have to hold him tight to stay on. His back to my chest and our thighs pressed together...

I definitely drank too much.

I'm already having the same thoughts that I had that night that we refuse to talk about.

Not a formal rule, but I'm sticking to not talking about it.

While I refuse to talk about it—he finds every opportunity to bring it up.

For somebody who's destined to forget that he was ever not a complete asshole to me, he sure thinks about what we did often enough.

Bentley's so warm in contrast to the cold leather underneath me.

I don't know why he chose to take his motorcycle tonight when February is still very much winter, but some part of me is happy to have the warmth near me. Even if it's only for a ride home since I'll be spending the rest of the night and weekend alone.

The last thing I wanted—sleeping alone again.

He spoiled that opportunity to find someone new, but he did keep me from that inevitable, *are you new in town* conversation, and even more awkward, *first of* conversations.

Even though he does irritate me, I know that I'm safely getting home from this club and no one harassed me...

And he smells like leather and oud...

If I close my eyes, then this could feel a little like the place I'm supposed to be. I rest my head on his back and let a little of the loneliness go, if only for this short ride.

There's a song about this... I know someone has written a song about riding a motorcycle with their man at night.

That freedom of being on the road with no restrictions. The wind on your skin. The buzzing vibration under your bodies.

Too lost in sensations, I open my eyes to notice that he's not taking the direction that would lead us to my flat.

He's going the opposite direction.

"Where are you going?" I yell over the roaring bike's engine.

"I'm hungry, so we're gonna go to The Diner first," he yells back.

Of course, he is.

Bentley just does whatever he wants.

Continue to ruin my night, why don't you?

We pull up to a stop light and I'm able to grumble, "Why can't you just do that after you drop me off?"

"Because it's the complete opposite direction of my condo. I'm not gonna drive thirty minutes out of the way just because I have baggage in tow."

Did he just call me baggage?

That asshole.

Chapter 11

Lee

We walk past the ATM machine through the narrow walkway between the booth and the serving counter. The warmth is more than welcome as the door swings close behind us.

Burgundy-red vinyl booths line one side of the diner, and Zadie plops into the second to last open seat. She immediately pushes the salt and pepper shaker in the condiment caddy to my side. Making room for her arms, she leans over the table.

I take my seat across from her, spreading my arms atop the back of the booth. A server called Tina places the two laminated menus in front of us. Zadie thanks her with a bright smile that Tina returns. I say nothing as I watch her try to look sober—an inebriated Zadie isn't far from a sober one. Both are a little too dreamy and lackadaisical to be taken seriously.

The extra large windows to my left allow for a few headlights to catch us every now and again as cars slowly drive by the main road. It's not as busy as it's ever been in this diner, but there are very few open seats at this time of night.

Likely because of the holiday.

Tina returns to ask for our order and I get a burger and fries. Zadie settles on a Cobb salad. I've never heard of a salad being the popular choice for someone who drank as much as she has, but I guess she knows her own mind. At least she's gonna stick with water.

She's happy to look out of the window while we wait for our food to come. Maybe her phone died or something. It surprises me that she's not on it. *There are many surprising things about this woman.*

What upsets me most is that I've been able to see that she is unlike what I expected. I make the assumption that I know what her next move will be and I'm blindsided by what she does anyway.

As social as she is and how willing she is to talk with everyone she meets, I would think that her presence online would be robust. Like maybe she has some sort of traveling influencer page or... I don't know, something. But she doesn't. Outside of the ancient profile she's had since we were all in school.

There is nothing.

I know. I've checked. It was only to find out what I could about her-not stalking her or anything. But her parents shared more online about her than she ever does.

She takes the photos, makes the trips but the only people she shares it with are her parents. And why?

If I had managed to do so much, I would tell anyone who wants to listen. Yes, I know I heard about it because Korra was always sharing or my Mom would.

Of the things she could brag about, her travels aren't actually one of them. Unless, I bait her, she doesn't actually share much.

Tina returns for a second time with our food and Zadie's attention is pulled back to the table. Her salad is huge on the plate in front of her. She makes quick work of mixing it and adding what she wants to it. It's a process that seems like way more work than it's worth. The only thing I have to do is pour a bit of ketchup for my fries to the side of the plate.

The silence is another guest at our table. The ambiance of food service hustle and murmur of conversation at other booths fill the space between us. I would say something, but I don't know what that could be.

She doesn't leave it up to me though. She shatters the quiet by asking. "Are you happy now?" Not only does she grab a fry from my plate, but she dips it into *my ketchup* like I've offered her fries, which I definitely have not. I reach for my fry before she's able to put it into her mouth, but she's quicker than me, chewing and continuing, "Now we're both alone on Valentine's Day. Was that your big plan?"

Look, I know it was a dick move to follow her to the club tonight. While my sister was grilling me about what I was going to do for this forsaken holiday she had let it slip that Zadie was going to the club tonight.

And that she wasn't going with a date.

If I were able to get over that night that we shared together and just move on to someone else, then I might have decided to stay home and let her do her thing-find some guy to go home with—have a good time.

Since I can't stop replaying how soft her skin was under my fingers or how lush her body was around me, then I couldn't let her have an opportunity to take someone home tonight.

I'll be damned if anyone is going home with her.

Maybe I just don't want to see her happy.

Maybe I just don't want to let her have any small victory leading up to the one that she's really going for.

Everyone knows that success is like a snowball. Once you get one you'll start getting others. If I let her win in this game in my mind, where she is taking up way too much space, then who knows what else she will succeed at?

The logic is flawed, but I can't reconcile it right now. It's far better to concentrate on this petty little feud that we've been fighting each other over than to really examine what's painful and obvious in front of me.

Zadie has grown up to become a woman who is capable of so much more than I'm willing to allow.

She could have handled herself at this club tonight by herself.

I knew that she would be able to find a way home if she really had gotten down to it.

But I also know that if anyone is going to take her home, it's going to be me.

Ever since the thought popped into my head I have not been able to let any other ones do such.

I take a bite out of my burger, chewing slowly as she narrows her eyes at me. The time I take in chewing irritates her, but she doesn't fill the space waiting for my reply. "We're not alone if we're together. So you're whining about nothing if we're talking about technicalities."

"*Whining*? Technicalities?" She balks as if I have said something that makes no sense. Then she takes another fry that I'm also not quick enough to grab out of her hand. Before she's done chewing, she says, "Who cares about technicalities when I'm stuck eating fries with you?"

In the light of the diner, I can see how good she looks tonight.

Her soft pink sweater makes the gold in her skin look even warmer. She's lit from within and there is no denying how that light is a draw to something brighter inside.

One of her shoulders is exposed to show the dog paw tattoo I've caught glimpses of on her arm.

And though we're sitting in the booth, I can still picture her hips filling out those tight jeans she has basically painted onto her body.

Her hazel-green eyes sparkle, even though now they're in challenge as I continue to hoard my fries.

Holding her challenging gaze, I inform her, "No one told you to eat my fries. I actually told you to order your own and you chose not to. I had no intention of sharing fries with you."

God, my life would be a lot easier if Zadie wasn't so beautiful.

My life would be a lot easier if I hadn't already known how she tasted.

My life would be a lot easier if Zadie wasn't constantly inserting herself into it.

And I guess here I am taking my position back by inserting myself first.

I run a hand over my face because inserting myself into Zadie's *anything* is not where my mind should be going if I expect to actually take her back to my sister's flat and not to my condo.

I make the mistake of looking away from my plate for one second and now I'm down another waffle fry.

"Oh, I see. You commandeered my Valentine's Day so that you didn't have to spend it alone." Zadie's eyes light with mischief. "All your siblings are booed up and there's just one person still here with no one to keep him company. Having troubles in the lady department, *Bent*?"

"Lee," I correct her. "And I'm not having troubles."

"So if you're not having troubles, then why is it that you have all this free time to spend with me tonight? I mean you're not bad looking. I'm sure if you tried, someone might be able to ignore your general stinky mood and give you a *little something*." She winks exaggeratedly with the last words with more finesse than I'd think she could even if she were sober.

"*My stinky mood*?" I raise an eyebrow. "Is that the best you've got? I feel like that's something you would've said when we were thirteen."

"What would you know about me at thirteen? You were hellbent on making me feel like enemy number one and criticizing my taste in music. And what do you know? Who is a K-pop fan now?" She scoffs before pushing her half-finished salad plate out of the way and leaning back in the booth. "Don't act like you knew anything about me back then."

Oh, I knew.

I knew a lot about her because she *was* enemy number one. I had to stay one step ahead of her in any way that I could because academically she was sweeping the floor with me. It was embarrassing every time I had to show up to get my ass handed to me by someone who didn't even seem like they were trying.

I take the last bite of my burger, letting what she's said hang in the air between us. "It was just a general statement, not reminiscing with you."

She's not placated by my words as she crosses her arms tightly. "Right. Because my memories of being thirteen are of me getting better grades than you, placing higher than you in every competition and also having to dumb down my arguments for debate class. Have I got that right?"

Pushing my plate away from me as well, I lean on to the table asking, "Why are you so determined to fight with me?"

Her cheeks turn a shade of red that is telling. With frustrated movements she bats the red curls away from her face. "Well, I could be fighting with someone else if you hadn't shown up tonight. As I mentioned before, I don't need to have an escort or a bodyguard. I know it's scary to be a woman in the world, but I have managed just fine for the past thirty-two years without you."

I don't know why that statement stings a little bit, but it does.

And that's dumb.

Frustrated by my confusion and words, I say the first thing that comes to mind. "I doubt that having to come home because you don't belong anywhere else counts as *managing just fine*."

I've got more than enough shit on my mind than to be thinking about what Zadie was doing with or without me. Or to pull my jealousy back about all the things that she was able to accomplish while I was making a mess of my life. *Taking everything in it for granted.* And now sitting in that same life without any of the things that I had once had.

Parents.

A relationship.

A career.

All of it dwindling away to nothing.

And the woman in front of me is already gaining two out of the three. Seeing her in a relationship when I can't be in one right now is too many W's for her team.

She rummages around in her oversized purse for a long while before producing her phone.

"What are you doing?" I ask as she swipes hurriedly on the screen.

"I'm going to find someone to take me home. I cannot be here with you for another minute."

My brows furrow. "What?" I ask and she continues swiping. "Just wait. I'm—" *Fuck*. "Look, I'm sorry. Zadie—"

"I don't want to hear it. The last time you apologized you made it much worse and I don't want to hear whatever undeserved bitterness you have for me."

Her phone begins to ring and she picks up. "Hey, Kase. What's—" She looks toward me while she listens to whatever my sister is saying on the phone. "Oh," she says. "No, it's not a big deal." She leans her head back, blowing out a long breath. "I'm sure. I'll catch up with you tomorrow." She slides out of the booth. "Okay, bye," she says, putting her phone back into her purse.

"Where are you going? What happened?" I question, after leaving some cash on the table for our food. "Zadie, wait," I call after her, but she is already by the entrance, shoving her arms into her coat.

I'm a few strides behind her though she isn't walking toward my bike. Her sleek brown boots crunch in the mixture of snow and gravel as she takes purposeful steps.

"Will you slow down? Zadie!"

"Stop following me," she snaps, her voice thick with emotion.

"No. I'm not going to do that. Let me just–will you slow down?" She's not that much shorter than me but she is quick in her boots and already paces ahead of me. "Please, let me just take you back to your flat."

"I can't," she begins. "I don't want to go back to the flat."

"Why?"

She shakes her head, biting her lip before responding, "I just don't. I'm going to my parents' house."

"No, you're not."

"I'm not?" She asks.

"No."

She blinks up at me in the street lamp illuminating the parking lot that we are on the edge of. "So, where am I going then?"

Chapter 12

Zadie

I can feel the light warming my face from the window, so I bury my head further into my pillow. It's a little harder than I remember, but the warmth is welcome. Snuggling my head deeper under the covers while I hold my pillow, I blink my eyes open and blink several more times before the deep rumble of a characteristically male chuckle rumbles against my cheek.

My sleepy voice is deeper than usual, which is not the squeal it very well could be. "Bentley, what are you doing in my bed?" I manage with a calm I don't feel.

Did I—

Did we—

No, *no*, *no*. This cannot be happening again.

My head throbs as I rub my bleary eyes to try and get my bearings a little better.

"You're in my bed, red." He gestures to the wall with his family photo on it. Details begin to come in clearer as I awake more fully. With a smirk, he states, "You called me Bentley."

"That is your name isn't it?" I snark, trying to check for my clothes as clandestinely as I can. It's no use when my heart starts beating faster.

This is not my very warm and cozy Valentine's appropriate sweater.

These are not my jeans.

No, *no, no*—

"Relax. Nothing happened last night. I offered you the couch, which you declined and demanded to sleep here instead. I gave you some clothes, but you were asleep before I even got out of the shower. Despite my king-sized bed, you move a lot in your sleep. Like, I might have a black eye from these wild fists you throw. I really don't remember that last time."

I cannot afford for last time *to happen again.*

There has been little to zero recovery from the last time. Figuring out what his problem is with me couldn't be further from my mind any more.

Especially now that my subconscious brain is sabotaging me by agreeing to come here and somehow sleeping in the same bed with him. That is the exact equivalent to dangling bacon in front of a hungry puppy.

This puppy is very hungry.

Ugh.

"Probably because I was actually exhausted," I mumble under my breath. *Ew—my breath.* I don't have a toothbrush or anything. I wasn't planning on staying the night at his house. I definitely wasn't planning on sleeping with him.

I *mean*, sleeping in bed with him.

Jeez.

Cuddling him for who knows how long.

"You just... You just let me cuddle you all night? Is this some sort of alternate dimension?" Awkwardly, I untangle myself from his sheets and stand on wobbly legs across from the man who is now sitting at the edge of his bed. He's not wearing a shirt and is only in thin pajama pants and glasses. Damn. Why do his legs still look so toned? And woah— I turn my head, but he didn't miss me checking what's between those toned legs out.

His morning voice is sinfully deep as he explains, "You were very active in your sleep." I can hear his annoying smirk in the tone of his sleepy voice.

"Oh, come off it, *Bent*!" I throw my hands in the air and I stomp towards the door that looks like it leads to a bathroom. "I didn't even remember where I was."

Good grief.

I look like a meatball.

My hair is an absolute chaotic mess all over my head. Flat on one side and tangled to be damned on the other. There is no stopping the beleaguered sigh that seeps from my lips. *There goes my entire day.* I'll be detangling and resolving this blunder. Couldn't drunk me have remembered to put on a bonnet or any one of the scarfs in my purse?

Damn.

I attempt to do something quickly about my head, turning on the water to rehydrate some of the curls. Privacy is not something Bentley affords me. He comes into the bathroom and leans against the wall behind me. He watches me fuss with my hair for a few minutes before he dares to open his mouth. "As much as I love the hair ball you're making in my sink, do you think you could hurry this up so that I can use the bathroom?"

I scoff instead of giving him a proper answer and stomp out of the bathroom. There has to be at least one more in this place. But nooo, he needed *me* to leave so that he could—

You know what? I've got to get out of here.

No memories come back to me about where I put all my things, but all I need is my purse, coat, and boots. I have got to get back home so I can assess the damage. Finding a hair tie and scarf in my purse, I throw my curls into some type of bun for the time being.

Before I can get my second foot into my boot, Bentley comes out of the room. "Where are you going now?"

"Home," I say, sliding the boot on.

He crosses his arms over his bare chest, making his pecks stand out even more. Stupid sleeper build. *Ugh.* "How are you getting there?"

"I'm going to walk, of course."

"Just like last night, I'm not going to agree to letting you walk that far. It's freezing. You're not dressed. Besides, the walk would take you almost two hours. Stop being a brat—"

"Me?" I exclaim, pointing at my chest. With my purse swinging wildly in the other hand, I say, "I am not the one who took someone to their house and made them sleep with them. Who does that?"

He closes the space between us with a couple of steps to give me the full weight of his gaze through his glasses. "I didn't make you do anything last night. *Nothing. Happened.* You are making a big deal out of absolutely nothing. I offered you a place to stay that wasn't in the throws of everyone else's romantic Valentine's evening and lost sleep over it because you're a goddamn MMA fighter once the consciousness goes. The only brat around here is you. I'll let you walk next time."

The frustrated little growl at the back of my throat is untethered before I can stop it. "You're not *letting* me do anything. Walking is one hundred times better than listening to you complain about problems of your own making." Grabbing my coat from the couch, I yank his door open and start heading the direction of my flat.

Getting my coat on, I already regret leaving, but there is no way in hell that I'm going back.

How could he blame me when it was him who crashed my plans last night?

No one told him to do that.

I actually said many times for him to leave me alone.

Ugh.

It's cold and windy this morning. The gust that rustles through my bones has to be going at least twenty miles-per-hour. I shiver down into my collar a little further and continue walking along the side of the road.

One car passes me without even slowing, but then another slows just behind me. I turn to catch a glimpse of who is following me and roll my eyes immediately before continuing on my trek.

"Zadie," Bentley calls from the open window next to me. His truck is quite a ways higher off the ground, so I have to look up at him to give him my glare and silence.

This is just a new adventure and challenge. I love both of those things. It's not even that cold...

As soon as I think it, another gust of wind blows by. I cross my arms even tighter, but it doesn't help me get any warmer. This February chill has not let up in the slightest.

"Where are those tights? They couldn't fit into your bag?" Bentley calls from the window as he keeps pace with me on the road.

"Jerk," I call out, foregoing ignoring him altogether. "Leave me alone. I'm making good time."

He laughs loudly. "To be there at dinner time."

I glare at him, then continue my march.

I will not get in his truck.

I'm not going anywhere with him ever again.

Another gust of wind pushes against me, making me stumble as the cold assaults my bare face.

Then, I stop walking.

A frustrated tear rolls down my cheek and I bat it away mostly so that it doesn't make me more cold. But also because I hate how weak it makes me look in front of him.

"Zadie. Please just get in." I know it makes sense to do what he says. It would be a quick fifteen minute ride that both of us could withstand.

I don't want to be vulnerable around him anymore though. I really don't want to give him this win. I don't have another choice. This man irritates me more that I could put into words, and yet I am always in his orbit.

Every choice I've made has led me back here. Back to him in some way or form.

I settle on the resolve that it doesn't mean that I will let up on him anymore than I already have.

I'm going after the veterinary position and there will be no room for softness and consideration if he's not willing to do the same.

As I reach for the door, I notice that there is music playing in the cabin. It's low but unmistakably PFP. He drives off as soon as I get buckled into my seat and turns the music up.

There is no way that he could know that this is my favorite album from them. And even still, no way that he could know that I listened to it every time I felt frustrated and alone. It was just random happenstance that this is playing.

It has to be.

It must be because I refuse to feel anything more than upset about the circumstance I'm in right now.

I'm going back to my flat like I've spent the night doing something far more pleasant than passing out in a spoiled nepo baby's arms.

When we arrive at the apartment building, I waste no time in getting out of his truck. Bentley calls after me, but I'm not willing to hear another word. I just want to get back home and forget about everything that happened over the last twenty-four hours.

Kasey is still in bed when I make my way up the three flights of stairs to our place.

There is no shower that could heal the hollow hole I feel in my chest after the night I had, but it at least makes me feel a little better to have a project to focus on.

For the rest of the day, I'm pampering myself.

Self-love never fails you.

Chapter 13

Lee

Long after I leave Zadie's place, I'm finally back at my condo. I took the long way home. By the long way home, I mean I finally went on that drive through the hills to get that picturesque view of my home town.

It's moments like this where it's unbearably quiet that I start to wonder about all the things that I am juggling in my mind. The one that screams the loudest at me is in an envelope on my coffee table.

I didn't have to put it away anywhere because no one visits me here. If the family gets together, it's either at my family's house or at Korra and Kasey's apartment, which makes a lot of sense. In this particular case, I know I've got nothing to worry about in terms of hiding.

My sisters are nosy as hell. Zadie, on the other hand, tends to only question what pertains to her and respects the boundaries that are unspoken. As odd as that might be, since it would likely behoove her to know what is in this envelope. It will likely destroy the last bits of my control.

When Zadie was here last night, I knew that I was in no danger of her finding anything because she wouldn't look. Though she might turn up everywhere, she isn't the type to go snooping through my things. Plus, she was in no state to be nosy when she could barely keep her eyes open.

Seeing her in my place, only for the brief time that she was here, had been a bit of a revelation. She walked around here like she already knew the place. *Like she was comfortable.* Even my ex, who had stayed here plenty of times, didn't move around that easily.

But I suppose that's Zadie's way.

She is welcome everywhere and everyone is a friend. She has no reason to feel self-conscious or awkward. As soon as she walked into my place, she went straight for the bedroom. There wasn't the thought of sitting on the couch or pretending to go for the cordial thing and offer to be a *polite guest*. It could be that she was still tipsy by the time we made it home, but I have a feeling she would be that way in either case if it weren't me—the man standing in the way of what she is trying to achieve.

But I am me.

I can't stop putting my foot in my mouth around her. I can't stop saying the wrong things and provoking her. The fire in her eyes as she challenges me is not something I want to let go of.

Where I know she is tough, I know she can be soft too. I don't deserve her softness or her ease.

She knows that, too.

It was a fight to get her on my bike from the diner and another to get her in my truck to take her home.

Knowing that she's where she's supposed to be now, I have to face the big pink elephant standing in my room.

It's been several weeks now since I went to retrieve this document from town hall and even still, it is one that I have been unable to open.

Today is the day though.

I have to get some answers.

There's been speculation, and I am fairly confident that I know the answer to the question that I've not wanted to receive. In either case if I wanna get any sort of resolution to what's going on in my mind, then I need to open this.

I take my time carefully lifting the top flap. I'm gripping this envelope so hard though I hardly doubt that this is where the damage would come from. I take a deep breath to release my grip and remove the papers.

On top is some sort of receipt, but just below that sheet is my birth certificate. The original.

Throughout my life, I somehow had never had to look at it. Either my Mom handled the paperwork or it was just unnecessary for me to have it. I had my social or a passport or any other sort of identification. But there it is. Or I guess I should say there it isn't.

My mother's name is right there, clear as day. But where the father area is, there's nothing.

It's completely blank.

I sit there for a moment just looking at the paperwork that is about to combust in my hand from how hard I stare at it.

I don't know what I expected to see here.

But I didn't expect *nothing*.

There is absolutely no mention of my father in this document.

And I guess when it comes down to it, I should have expected nothing.

My siblings don't want me to address my Dad about this. But he had to know. He had to have known my whole life. And just like my Mom, he never told me the truth.

So now this idea of *who in the hell is Aidan Kendrick* is an even more glaring alarm ringing through my mind.

Who is this man?

And how did my Mom know him?

It's times like this where I wish I had someone to talk to about my Mom. I'll never know what her true intentions were in keeping this from me. It hurts more to know that this entire time she had been keeping this close to her chest, and I had been none the wiser.

I had felt like the only one who was not like everyone else, because I was the only one unlike everyone else in the family. Because of a choice that she made, I had worked harder than everyone else to try and be the best and the brightest.

My siblings thought that I was getting preferential treatment. Like my Mom was never as hard on me as she was with everyone else. And though I disagree that she was not hard on me— she had treated me differently. She was softer with me.

Had that softness come from guilt at this huge secret?

Had her affection for me been genuine, or just an act of consolation for the lies she had told?

The best people to talk about this would be Korra, Kasey, Zach and Nia. But they've made it clear that they would rather protect whatever delicate emotional state my Dad is in than resolve the issues that I'm fighting with.

The man they're trying to protect is just as culpable as my Mom was.

And in a small town like this?

How did she get away with it?

What was the reason for her having an affair?

And why is my Dad not more upset?

The only two people who truly know what went down are gone. My Dad is still here mourning the loss of a woman who had to have cheated on him and had a child with another man.

I don't know whether to be pissed off or depressed.

I don't know who to talk to about this. I don't even know how to feel. Because at the end of the day, I did have a father figure in my house. I did have a Dad. *I do have a Dad.* And though our relationship is contentious right now because I've been abnormally cranky due to having a parental crisis at the ripe age of thirty-two, he has been in my life this whole time.

I don't agree with the choices that he's making as of late, especially in regards to who's going to succeed him. And if I really hated it, I could work anywhere else.

How depressing is it to know that you couldn't even land a vet job at your own family's clinic?

What does that say about me?

What does it say about him?

In all these circumstances, I still look like the ass. And I don't know why it upsets me now that I look like the ass. And I think maybe it upsets me even more because I look like shit and Zadie looks like the fucking hero.

Why does she get to be the hero?

What makes her so fucking special?

And that's a whole different line of questioning I don't want to go down because I know the answer to that question. There's so many answers to that question. All of which I don't want to acknowledge.

Though I might be the only Thomas sibling who isn't a true Thomas sibling.

A half sibling is still way closer to family than a complete stranger.

It doesn't matter anyway.

This is still a fight.

I still have a chance and I refuse to let Zadie win this time around.

Chapter 14

Zadie

After my call with Wayne, it had definitely hit home to Bentley that I was much further along in gaining, not only, the trust but approval from Wayne. Moving forward with this contest that we have, I had a brief moment of happiness.

I mean, who wouldn't be smug at besting the person that has been an actual thorn in their side for months? I guess not me because as soon as he left, I knew something was going on. I had so many opportunities to talk to him and figure out exactly what was with his unusually icky mood.

I get that people have hard weeks.

I get that people have hard lives.

But I know the Thomas family and I see him almost every day and I just can't figure out what it is that makes him so sour. To me it doesn't seem like it's just a personality thing.

Yes, there are people who are actual assholes, but when I lived here before I remember there were times where he was joking–where he was smiling.

Even still at the clinic, I can see him have a good time when he gets certain patients that he likes seeing.

There is something going on with him...

And I don't want to care, but I do.

I know there's something more. I just don't know what to do about it.

After all that's said and done, I still am in charge of putting together an adoption event in the next two weeks.

I know what goes into one. But I've honestly never planned one myself. I would ask Korra to hop on this since she is definitely far more adept at event planning than I am. But she is planning a much more important event for her. I want her to have full focus on her wedding. Especially not after I had already said that she shouldn't be bothered, when I was mouthing off to Bentley.

The short notice equates to a struggle for even an experienced event planner. I am not experienced. I'm not going to be able to do this on my own.

What sucks the most is that I'm going to have to talk to him.

I'm going to have to make him more involved in this than I wanted to. Honestly, I just don't think I have the mental capacity to take on this whole event by myself. I'm sure there are other people I could ask.

If he wants to have a fair shot of this then he's gotta have a fair shot at the work too.

God, if we team up then that means we'll have to *work together*. Which means that he'll probably be in a shitty mood and have an even shittier attitude because he feels like he has won something by me having this ask of him.

I wish there was someone I could talk to you about this.

I'm going to have to bite the bullet and just call Korra. I'll make it super clear that she's not to get involved in planning, but I do need some sort of guidance. She's gonna have some insight that she can give that does not actually require her to become a part of this situation...

Right?

Before I call her, I need to see my Mom.

Walking in the large studio, my Mom is already sitting on a mat in the middle of the studio floor. I ask into the open space, "Are you busy?"

She doesn't flinch, just exhales to respond, "No sweetie, I'm just meditating for a bit. Do you want to join me?"

"No, I don't need meditation right now." I sit next to her on a mat anyway.

"What about groceries. Have you done that yet?" The last thing I told her was that I didn't have any in the flat over texts.

I sigh. "I am gonna have to start doing my own grocery again. Not looking forward to it. That's not why I came here though. I kind of have this work thing that I took on..."

Mom twists at the waist over her right leg to face me. "Okay. What kind of work thing?"

"Well I kind of said that I was going to help with the spring pet adoption... You know? Hosting it."

On her exhale she twists the opposite direction. "As in the biggest adoption event that happens in Harmony Hill every year..."

"Oh, so you've heard of it?" There's no way she hasn't heard of it. Since it is the biggest adoption event of the year. Her daughter is absolutely obsessed with animals. Has been her whole life and usually attends to see the animals.

Of course she's heard of it.

She confirms as much, "Yes, princess, I have heard of it. Why is it that you're hosting it and not the Brenford family like they always do?"

My next words come out on a single breath with my nerves. "Well, I'm not really sure what's happening there, but the Thomases were always involved and since I work at the clinic, I suggested that I would help organize it, so that I could potentially get ahead in the running that I have with Bentley right now to be the next vet at the clinic..."

You know, saying this out loud does make me sound a little bit more delusional than I had previously assumed. *I am definitely in over my head.* But I can make this event happen. I could do a damn good job too. At least I think I can.

No, I know I can. I just need a little guidance...

"Well, I think it's fantastic that you took some initiative here. It does sound like you're having a great time back in Harmony Hill so far, which I love," she hedges. "But don't you think this is maybe too big a thing to have just one person doing all of the planning for? What is Wayne doing to help?"

"Well, you see that's the thing. I told him that I would get it all handled and if there's anything I needed help with I would find the resources. The clinic is paying for everything. I have to get it put together. Couldn't see this event fall to the wayside. *People look forward to this.* If not to find their new best friend, but to also support the community. There's a lot of fundraising."

"And that's all very admirable sweetie. Truly, it is. Have you thought about the fact that you have never planned an event this size or really any event in your life? This is probably not the first one to try your hand at." She winces a bit, "Though I do believe in you and I think that you would do an amazing job."

"Well, I'm not gonna do it all by myself. Bentley's gonna help," I say with the conviction of someone who's already talked to Bentley and he's already agreed—which I have not and he has not. "And we still have the rest of the clinic to help with things, as well. I just have to get everything organized. I came to see if you thought that I could do it and it kind of sounds like you're doubting me."

"I believe you can do anything you put your mind too, princess. You wanted to travel the world and look at what you did. Just that." She reaches for my hand and I let her take it. "I don't doubt that anything you want to achieve you can. There must be easier ways to secure a veterinary position, right?" I cut her a look and she rubs my arm. "I'm not gonna stand in your way of anything you want to do, but I do wanna be a voice of reason in saying that you might want to get a book or two."

This visit did not give me the reassurance I was seeking. "I'm not getting a book. It's gonna be fine. I'm going to just collaborate and it'll be a good event."

I'll have to call Korra at another time, I've got to get this off my mind for a while.

Returning to my flat with groceries in hand, something hits me. It's been years since I've lived somewhere that I know I'm going to be at for a long time. I have lived in many places for several months at a time, don't get me wrong. But all of those places had only minimal decorations or I just used things that I got in my everyday life to put around the space, but this is completely different.

I have a flat.

I have a roommate.

I have a career track that will end with more stability than I've ever had in my adult life.

And I intend to make this space look exactly how I want a *Zadie flat* to look. Now, I have to decide what that means.

I don't think that I'm a painted wall kind of person, but I do know that I'm going to unapologetically dedicate a wall to my favorite band—Past, Present, Future or PFP. I finally have a place to put all of the albums, posters and little merchandise that I've gathered over the years, even from being a teenage fan. I'm thankful that my Mom kept the box of things that I had in my room when I was younger.

The fact that they are a group that continues to make amazing music is mind-boggling and also an incredible feat. I can't believe that Bentley, of all people, actually listens to their music. The song that played in the ice rink the other day was not even a new song. So it kind of makes me wonder how long he's been a *Time Traveler*, that's what fans of PFP are called.

I'm sure there's plenty of things I don't know about him. He's such a grouchy grumpy mess. It seems like if you ask him any questions or get too close to seeing below the surface, he freaks out and just starts being the worst. Outside of the general unpleasantness that he shows towards me, I think that is the case, regardless. I don't know if he even has friends outside of his family.

Wouldn't surprise me if he doesn't.

After I put the grocery away, I go back to my room and figure out two things.

One, how am I going to decorate my new place?

Two, how am I going to swallow my pride to ask Bentley to join planning this event with me?

Chapter 15

Lee

I know that my sister has more information than she's letting on. All I've gotta do is see what she's up to. The only thing is—I'm not sure how much information I'll be able to squeeze from her if her fiancé is there.

I'm just gonna have to take my chances because if there's anybody who will have the best advice on what to do next in this circumstance, it would be Korra.

The drive to Korra's house is definitely one that I would recommend if you're looking for some of those stereotypical Coloradan views. The Long county road that leads to my sister's new house is everything that makes this state beautiful.

Row upon row of ever growing mountain ridges, the hills are just the first steps to them. You can even see the outlines of some of the larger peaks before the ones behind it that disappear into the clouds.

I don't know what Bryce did to be able to score this house, but to say I'm jealous is an understatement. One day, I'll move out of my condo to a home of my own. It has a pretty decent view of the mountains, but oftentimes is obstructed by people's trees. There isn't much property to speak of. I've been living in the same place since I graduated and came home. I knew pretty quickly that I wasn't gonna be able to live in the house with my family. I love them, but I need my space—and my quiet. It seems like the overwhelming majority has their positivity meter turned all the way to the max limit. I don't mind a little bit of that every now and again, but for the most part, I'm not trying to see the bigger or brighter picture.

I better accept that for the next hour or so that's what I've got coming.

Korra isn't what I would say the brightest of bright lights, but she does have an overwhelmingly positive outlook on just about anything. And if it comes to the family, she has a way of spinning it positively–no matter what the case is. Bryce seems to do a little bit of the tempering on that and adding in the realism that she desperately needs, but if he can see that anything I'm doing is upsetting her, he might kick me out. Whereas I wouldn't mind getting kicked out any other time, today, I'm not looking for that sort of outcome.

Before I can get my second knock on the door, Bryce opens it and I'm standing there face-to-face with him. "You came without calling?"

"I didn't realize I needed to call ahead to see my own sister."

He crosses his arms over his chest, still standing in the doorway. His expression isn't unpleasant, but it isn't welcoming either. "Maybe at your parent's house or at the flat, but here where we're fiancés... You might get an eye full of something you don't wanna get an eye full of if you just traipse your ass through here like you own the place."

"First of all–gross. That is my big sister. I understand you guys are doing, whatever it is you're doing, but geez, it's fucking midday."

"Exactly, and I would like to spend my weekend doing the things I like best–which is your sister. And I want it to be as uncomfortable for you as possible now, so that you don't make the mistake in the future. As soon as we're newlyweds, we might put up a gate before you can even park in this place."

Holding my hands up in front of me, I concede. "Okay, message received. Am I in any danger of seeing something I don't wanna see you now?"

"Now, you're good." He claps me on the back and ushers me inside, finally. I immediately kick off my boots and enjoy the warmth of their new house.

If I had been outside for even a few minutes longer I might have abandoned my cause. It's still freezing out.

I haven't been here since they moved in. It really does look like a house Korra would live in. Already there's greenery cluttering the walls, tables, and any available surface. There's even a few hooks where various plants are dangling just like it was at the flat before Korra moved out.

Korra comes from somewhere deeper in the house to exclaim, "Lee! This is a good surprise. I haven't seen you since Thursday... When we were at work. What brings you to here?"

"Is that sarcasm?" I look towards my future brother-in-law. "Are you teaching my lovable sister *sarcasm*? I didn't realize you would be such a bad influence."

"Any sarcasm she's giving you–you've earned on your own. It's been years that I've been trying to get her to use it and she very rarely does so..."

I scowl, not liking what he's trying to imply. "What did I do?"

Korra shrugs before plopping onto her couch. "Besides giving my good friend a hard time, per usual, I'd say nothing. You definitely have earned some sarcasm, baby bro."

"There's my point," Bryce agrees and sits next to his fiancé.

Great.

A double team I'm used to from the twins, but now Bryce has taken Kasey's place.

"This is actually perfect," Korra says. "I'm working on the next page in our scrapbook. And last time you said you were too busy, but you've got so much time on your hands today. We could work on a spread together. How about it?"

Internally, I'm cringing because I should have known that she would be doing some sort of project. I was hoping it'd be more of the gardening variety. *Not arts and crafts.*

I do need to have her unguarded and willing to talk about what she found the last time that she was creating a scrapbooking spread. So with my very best and most convincing smile, I say, "Sure. Why not?"

Following her to the second floor, we enter a room I've not been in before. She has all types of things laid out. It seems like almost a replica of Mom studio with the shelving that she must've moved out of the studio into this room. All the shelves are lined with boxes that I know are filled with all types of paper crafting supplies.

"Ah! Mind Valentino," she says when I brush the trailing leaves out of my way. The overstuffed chair in the corner is the main difference between Korra's room and Mom's studio. There is no piano or instruments of any kind in here. Instead, there are more plants. The one I just moved off of the chair back has big heart-shaped leaves in a pink and red glossy pot on the stool it sits on.

"Who is Valentino?"

"The Philodendron hederaceum you nearly sat on. He's very particular about his space."

The plant. "Right. Okay." I slide the stool over so that I don't damage this thing that I know she cares about enough to give a human name. Mom gave Korra the green thumb, but this is exceeding Mom's obsession for sure.

"Since winter is almost over and I haven't had a chance to do one, I think we should do a winter themed spread. There are lots to choose from."

I have nothing to add, choosing to let her lead this project. I've got a different goal in mind.

She starts spreading out pattern papers, all types of gadgets that I have no idea what they do, and even more stickers with various types of effects. Some are layered and pop out, some have jewels on them, some puffy–I just start grabbing the ones that call to me.

There is a smaller box that Korra opens and begins to flick through. It's all photos in this box. She settles on one but I don't recognize which of the twins I'm looking at because the little girl in the photo is smiling.

"Who is that?" I ask.

"Why it's me, baby bro," comes Kasey monotone from the doorway. I hadn't even heard her coming upstairs or into the house for that matter.

"I'm really not liking this *baby bro*," I grumble.

Kasey shrugs, taking a seat on the floor beside Korra. "You act enough like a baby that it seems to be the most appropriate nickname for you. It's at least a little better than the ones Zadie's giving you right?"

"Marginally."

Kasey smirks, "So, what are we working on?"

"I was just telling Lee that we should do a winter themed spread. Mom's got so many pretty papers and... Look at these little poinsettias!" My sister affectionately holds up a sticker that has the red flowers on them. That makes me think of the arrangements that Korra had around the house on the night Zadie and I hooked up.

I'm stuck reminiscing about my time between Zadie's thighs while my sisters continue the conversation around me.

"Yeah, but Valentine's Day really wasn't that long ago. You should add in something from that," Kasey says.

"Oh, that's a really good idea. Valentine's Day always calls for roses," Korra tells her.

"Is that what Bryce got you?" Kasey asks.

"No, he did one better," Korra beams. "He planted an entire row of rose bushes in the backyard. They're gonna bloom so beautifully this summer. I might be able to use them in my bouquet."

Okay, I've got to steer this in a different direction. *That's why I came over here after all.* The fact that Kasey's here maybe is a little better for my goals.

I scratch the back of my neck and sit a little straighter in my seat. "You moved all of Mom's stuff in here. Have you found anything else?"

My sisters look at each other before long-haired one calls me out on the abrupt change in topic.

"Really smooth transition," Kasey says. "If you must know, I've read a couple more journals that she left." Korra gives her a sharp look that Kasey glosses over, saying, "What? She didn't do anything to protect the evidence of what she had been into. I mean, there's not even, like a lock on them nor did she put them in a lock box. At least the box you found that ID in had a latch on it. These are wide open on her shelf... and they're basically illustrated with how fond she was on including photos. Mom lived a very colorful life. Which I have now taken into the inspiration for an epic story. I have no idea what it's going to be, but I will say that she left so many amazing questions to explore literarily."

"Kase, you write romance," Korra says.

"Exactly! I'm going to write the story about the love that never was and the man she chose. Very *The Notebook*-esque."

Korra balks again. "*The Notebook* ended with a tragedy. I don't even know if that's considered romance."

"It isn't considered romance. I just said that it was like that. And I didn't say that was exactly how I was going to write the story. I just said it reminded me of that circumstance."

All this talk of *The Notebook*—I don't know what the fuck that is. But she said romance... And no mention of my Dad—well, of Wayne. "So you found more stuff about Aiden?" I ask.

"Oh yes! Tons! Their story was actually very sweet. But, of course like I said, a little bit tragic. Although, I'm guessing it's a lot tragic. Considering she married Wayne and not Aiden," Kasey says.

"What does that mean?"

"Well they grew up together. They were sort of singing rivals for a time. They both did a lot of performing. They appeared in multiple musicals together. She really talks about him fondly. It was a friendship that was over a decade long considering they, like, went to elementary, middle and high school together." Kasey leans back on her hands while her twin continues organizing materials to decorate this scrapbook spread. "I mean, he ended up going away to the military and I'm guessing that's when Mom met Wayne. Then the story is really changed. She loved Dad, that much is so clear. But I'm guessing when Aiden was done with his enlistment—things changed." Her eyebrows raise as she looks at me.

The more Kasey talks, the more confused I am. "What do you mean things changed?"

"Well in the journal that I read most recently, it talks about the show that the Brenfords and Kindricks put on when he came back. Both of them were still well-known singers in the community and they did a performance together. It doesn't look like they did many more after that though. She doesn't talk about any other performances with him... or seeing any performances of him. Mom tends to detail the shows that she sees quite often in these journals. It's really beautiful to hear how she talked about music and performance—especially of others. She doesn't talk loads about herself, but she does do a lot of detailed accounts of what she really loved in the musicals or in concerts she's assisted in or viewed casually. It's very cool. Interesting how the mind works."

So my Mom talked about this man in these journals.

In just a few minutes I was able to learn more about my birth-father than I had found on my own. Granted I wasn't looking *that hard.*

But I had no idea that he was in the military.

Or that he was a singer.

I wonder if his voice sounded like mine and if that's why my Mom always wanted me to pursue singing so she could hear his voice again.

Cause if he passed...

She no longer had a relationship with him...

They were close at one point, obviously, here I am...

If I sound like him that would be wild.

"Oh, you know what would be so special?" Korra asks. "What if we could find a video of them singing together? That would be so cool." I don't know how she's hearing my thoughts but it's freaky. Maybe I've tapped into that twin connection Korra and Kasey share.

"I mean, I guess it will be cool," I say with as much nonchalance as I can manage though I'm very curious to hear. "But it would be a little weird, especially, because you know? Who he is..."

Discomfort is written on the lines of Korra's forehead and she asks, "Do you think that would be disrespectful to Dad or something?

"Why would Dad care? I mean, he did win out in this romance. He's just like James Marsden's character. And I guess Ryan Gosling's character was Aiden..."

Korra shakes her head, "Oh my gosh this is gonna be so messy. Forget, I said anything."

"No, no, no, no, no. This is exactly what I live for. You don't have to watch it if you don't want to, but I'm one-hundred percent going to look for a video of them together. I mean it was the nineties, maybe somebody has a record of this. I wonder who would..." Kasey trails off as she searches on her phone.

Nerves make my hands shake. "Korra's right. Maybe we should—"

"Ha!" Kasey exclaims. "Found it. It was televised by local news. Apparently there were a lot of veterans in this show." She turns her phone so that the video is full screen. The three of us gather around it to see what she's seeing. "Look at Mom, she's so beautiful."

"Turn the volume up so I can hear," Korra says.

There is still a lot of commentary as the host announces what they are on stage for, but the ringing in my ears is loud until I hear them taking the lead in this performance.

My suspicions were true.

As soon as they began singing the duet opening lines, I recognize that his voice and mine are very similar.

Them singing together sounds like my Mom and I singing together.

Everything about this moment between them seems so much deeper than reconnecting with an old friend. I could not have connected the dots any more clearly. Seeing him animated and alive on this phone screen is too much to bear. This is far worse than seeing his picture. Aiden Kindrick can only be one person to me. How could no one see that before?

It seems like my sisters are really starting to see it as well. They both look at me with glassy eyes. It's not often that my sisters share emotions like this. I mean, they are twins and often sometimes they have that freaky identical twin thing, but this is too much.

I need some space and some air.

Getting up, I walk to the window and just stare out of it as my eyes sting to match the ringing that has intensified in my ears.

With a hand over her mouth, Korra stands to walk towards me, but I hold out a hand. My emotions are in a tangled mess right now.

Of course Kasey says the thing that no one else will. "You have to figure out what happened. I don't know how we would go about doing that. I still think it's important that you don't involve Dad, but this is unreal. I mean it's like looking at a lighter version of you in the past. I used to think you had Mom's hair, but really his hair is only slightly less curly than yours. I mean in your face–your voice." With an unwavering gaze, Kasey faces me with no humor or sarcasm. "I mean this in the most unironic way possible, because I feel like I'm an authority in the matter. You two are twins."

I've got to get out of here. It's imperative that I leave before I blow up on them and neither of them deserve it.

I'm down the stairs when Bryce calls my name. On a dedicated path to my truck, I still hear his words. "Lee! We need to talk! Lee—"

Down their porch steps I go.

Back to my condo.

Back to when I didn't know what my birth-father sounded like.

Back to when my biggest problem was a spunky redhead.

Chapter 16

Zadie

Hard to believe that February has flown by. It is the shortest month in the year, but for whatever reason, it feels shorter. I know that has everything to do with Bentley Thomas.

After a very confusing Valentine's Day, I'm even more disoriented than before. At work, it should be a breeze. With the impending adoption drive looming overhead, my daily tasks and paperwork are feeling more tenuous. It is important now, more than ever, to be on top of every little detail though. Gloating in Bentley's face put me in the worst position to ask him for help.

Sure, Z. Move back to your hometown. Reacquaint yourself with the boy who thinks you're the villain and he's the hero. Sleep with him, intimately and otherwise. Piss him off. Oh, and then turn around to ask him to help you.

Really great plan.

Who left me in charge?

Oh, right. I asked for this.

Harmony Hill is supposed to be my home base. Returning back to the nest is over. I'm an adult now. Like a real one. Job, own place, and the like.

So, why do I feel like the teenage girl who needed someone desperately to see her?

The worst he can do is say no.

Right?

Tossing what's left of my wrap into the trash, lunch time is over since Wayne has paged me to assist him. I go up front to greet the woman here with her floppy Golden Retriever. "Oh, a precious puppy," I say, bending to see the sweet girl in her frilly yellow collar. Her tag reads *Sunny*. "Sunny, you are so beautiful." She nips all over my hands with her little puppy teeth as I rub her.

I've always had a soft spot for Goldens though I haven't had one since I lived here last. The memory of him resides on my shoulder. With my traveling it just wasn't feasible to have a pet. Now that I've moved back home, I might change my outlook on that stance. I have a place of my own, it's a possibility unlike before. Sunny is too cute.

When we get to the room, I begin setting up a treat for her once the vaccines come out. In the meantime, I keep her busy or still depending on what Wayne needs as he looks over her health and condition. He talks to Sunny's owner, Tasha, as I enjoy the brief moments of puppy loving.

"We're going to get her vaccines done, now," Wayne tells Tasha. "I'll be quick and she probably won't even notice." He nods his head toward me as I put a couple of treats on the table with a slow feeder. There isn't much here, but a dog her age isn't quick enough to outsmart the feeder before Wayne gets the shots done.

I hold her under the belly with my arms, which ends up being more like a hug as Sunny can't decide if she wants my kisses or the treats more. She doesn't even flinch, much too engrossed in the soft food she licks up.

I get Sunny ready to go as Wayne talks with Tasha out to the front desk again. "Come back to see me next year," I call out to Sunny and Tasha before I return to the back. Tasha gives me a wave and Sunny lets out a little yip just before I'm around the hall.

Several hours have passed before I see Wayne again as I've got my own appointments. Just before the end of the day, he catches me walking toward the front desk.

"How are you doing?" he asks. The question is innocuous enough but I sense a different conversation on the horizon. I've known Wayne Thomas since I was a young kid. Though we're past the formalities, I still look up to this man. As a young person, he was the only person of color that I knew who owned and ran a successful business in the industry that fascinated me. He was the recommendation everyone gave for a good vet in town. There is another clinic just on the outskirts, but Thomas & Friends earned their reputation from the man walking with me now. He may be decades older than he was when I brought my dog in for his first appointment, but he is still the same competent and amenable man I've known.

"I'm doing alright. It's hump day though so I'm hanging in there."

"Oh. Yes, yes. Hump day," he says, distracted-like before stopping in the hall.

"Is there something you wanted to talk about?" I ask, hoping to get to whatever is going on here.

He scratches the white stubble on his jaw briefly. "The adoption drive. How is that going?"

I brush a hand down the front of my scrubs. "I've got some things in order, but I'm still working diligently on organizing."

"That's good. I've given more thought to traveling and I think I'd like to go to Morocco. All is looking good, but I don't want to leave you all in the lurch with my parting."

As much as it pains me to say something positive right now about Bentley I know that Wayne is not feeling confident with his son's unpredictable behavior. "Bentley and I are more than capable of holding down the fort so that you can enjoy some peace."

He nods and begins walking again. "Glad to know that my son hasn't completely ruined our chances of holding on to you," Wayne comments, just as we reach the opening for Korra's desk.

Without prompting my friend says, "She wouldn't let Lee get to her. Zadie doesn't need his approval to do anything."

"That's right," I say with a smile because she's right. I don't need anyone's approval for anything. Especially not from a spoiled nepo baby who has absolutely no reason to have such a shitty attitude toward me. If I need him to help with this pet adoption, that is not the same as giving up my position in the lead.

When I was working abroad, growing my experience in helping animals wherever I could with the organization I joined, I had so many options for what I could do afterward. I could work anywhere in the world and had done so. I'd seen places I had only dreamed of and supported myself well while doing it.

"Except she does need my help to set up the chemistry machines in the morning," Bentley says, coming to join us at the front desk. "Both tables are ready for surgery and sedatives have been administered," he says to his Dad.

"I know that's not true," Wayne says in my defense, giving his son a stern look.

"They are though... Feel free to check," he says, purposefully misunderstanding Wayne's meaning.

I've not had anyone give me a hard time nearly as much as Bentley does. I've looked up to Wayne and this clinic has always been a place I could see myself working. All that I'm going through though... Is it even worth it?

My boss doesn't comment on it, "I'll get back there to get started."

"This is exactly what Dad was talking about," Korra says to her brother.

Now is as good a time as any. Having my friend here as a witness should things turn ugly is not a bad circumstance either. Especially since he is already trying to make me look bad, but I have to get this out of the way. *The worst thing he can do is say no.*

With Wayne firmly out of earshot, taking a deep breath in, I exhale the question so I don't chicken out. "This adoption event is a very big deal for the clinic. As such, there needs to be more than one person overseeing it so that Wayne can continue to enjoy the time off he is taking." It's not really a question. I haven't actually asked anything, but I hope that Bentley will take the hint and understand anyway.

His eyes twinkle with mischief and I know he understands. "Oh, yes. It is a very big deal. It must go off without a hitch."

I pin Bentley with a look. "The only way this is going to work is if we work together. Do you think that you can manage that?"

He leans down so that he's speaking directly in my face. His breath smells of mints as it whispers over my cheeks in contrast with the snark of his words. "I can manage, but I'm not doing it for you." Straightening, he adds. "I'm doing it because I do care about my Dad's legacy whether or not he believes that I do. And though I am the rightful successor for his legacy, I won't see his name be run through the mud because you weren't able to do it right."

Rolling my eyes as I throw my hands in the air, I exclaim in as low a voice as I can while still communicating how annoyed I am. "For heavens' sake, *Bent*, could you have not just said yes? You just had to give this whole mumbo-jumbo ass, long-winded response. A simple yes or no would've been fine."

His arms cross over his chest making the short sleeves stretch over defined biceps. "It's not too late for me to turn around..."

God, I hate how this has turned for me. "No, no, no. Fine. If we're gonna work together, then I agree to not complain about how long-winded you are with everything."

With eyes rolling he huffs, "Gee, thanks."

Honestly, I can't help but tease him because he is insufferable most times. *An easy target is an easy target.* "And in order for that to happen, you're going to have to be honest with me. Does the stick go right up or does it taper off at some point."

"Okay, I'm leaving," Bentley says, as he turns for the hallway.

I place a hand on his arm to stop him from turning around. "I'm just kidding. But you do need to learn to lighten up. This event is going to be fun and, even though you've never shown me that you know how to do that, I trust you know what it looks like right?"

"I'd said I'd help. Not that I'd stick around for you teasing me," he says on his way back out.

"Fine, Mr. Grumpy pants," I call to his retreating back.

It's not until I'm in Lemon, driving home that I reflect on the day. Seeing Daisy earlier really made me think about Oliver. It's not uncommon for any veterinary professional to adopt their own animal companions, but I've not had the opportunity since I never knew how long I'd be in any given place.

After my first dog passed when I was in high school, there was no thought of getting another dog after that. Not seriously anyway. I'd miss him too much. The one and only tattoo I have is an outline of his paw print with his birth flower interwoven in the thin lines. It makes me smile thinking about him every time I see it.

The stability I crave is never going away. It's not a whole destination like any of my trips in the past. It's a feeling that no matter where I looked, it evaded me. With all my might I'm looking for a place that I can call mine and mean it.

Every single time that I think—hey, Harmony Hill feels like home again, there is something to snatch that feeling away. Somehow it's usually Bentley shaped, today, it's commitment shaped.

After all I've been though I still have to rely on him to help me because I don't feel that I can do it on my own. I might not be enough to host this event. It's silly because there was never one person who hosted it in the past, but defeat tastes bitter on my tongue as I walk into my flat and crawl to my shower after this long day.

Coming home to a wagging tail and unconditional love doesn't sound too bad, but stability isn't quite in my grasp as I settle into a nighttime yoga flow to relax before bed.

I'm watching a documentary about whale migrations when my phone buzzes on my nightstand. I'm not expecting anyone, so I reach over in case it's an emergency.

Not an emergency, but a cause for alarm either way.

He is texting me late at night.

Bentley: We've got less than two weeks to do this. What have you done so far?

Well, initiative is not unwelcome. I just wish it was a little different.

No, hi.

No, how are you?

Zero formalities when it comes to this man.

Zadie: I'll show you what I've got covered. Are you free this weekend?

Bentley: Sure. I can be.

Here we go.

Chapter 17

Lee

With our agreement to work together on this event, Zadie invited me to a café in the Hills. Little does she know that I'm a frequent patron of this establishment because it is the perfect halfway point from my scenic drives and my condo.

It also holds a special place in my heart.

The building seems to be nestled right in the side of the cliff face. During cherry season, they set up a stand right outside to sell their signature cherry pie and pie filling. I remember the first time my Mom brought me here and let me sample every cherry treat they had to offer until I had gorged on more than my fair share.

Last year, I wasn't able to go with her and I had to bring her pie to the hospital. Her appetite had already gone by then, so she wasn't able or willing to take more than a bite before we ended up just sitting together.

I push aside the memories that make me pity the woman who was larger than life. My emotions are complicated enough as it is. I don't want to remember her as the woman she withered away to. I want to remember her as the vibrant personality whose voice carried farther than sound.

Many of her kindnesses still ring in this community. *Many of them still resonate in me.*

Pushing the distrust and resentment that has grown from discovering her secret is hard when it impacts me more than anything else. Her secret could easily tarnish my feelings toward her. Though it's difficult, I'm trying my hardest to keep that picture in my mind of her untarnished.

Parking on the side opposite of where the stand is usually located, I walk inside to find the woman with large, red hair and big, green eyes waiting at the table right by the front door. The view from the window is the best in the spot she's chosen. The opposite cliff stretches up and trees are thick though bare. There may be a few short weeks before that changes with Spring fast-approaching.

"You're just like a cat," I say as I take the seat across from her. "You're always in a window."

Her eyes snap to me and she sips from a tea cup before responding, "Only house cats do that. I don't think I'm anything like a house cat."

Her assessment has intrigued me. I expected her to balk, but this response is thoughtful and honest. Not instigating.

"No? What do you think you're like?"

"I'd say I'm more like an outdoor cat," moving hair from her face, she expands, "They like to explore and roam, but eventually come back to the place they recognize as safe—home. That can change depending on the animal, but overall, an outdoor cat will follow that predictable pattern for its whole life. They'll always want to leave and feel free, but they are distressed when they don't have a place to lay their heads at night."

"That's true," I watch the cars driving by on the curved road outside the window. It's curious to me that this is the comparison she has for herself. I didn't expect her to feel this way or treat my flippant comment as one with any merit. She continues to surprise me. Looking her over, I note her coordinating lounge set and sneakers. "They take good care of themselves, often having the best health in comparison to the indoor cats we see. Maybe it has something to do with all the exercise."

"Or the free will," she says simply, sipping from her cup again. She's no longer entertaining my musings and getting right to business. "We've got a lot to cover. I've put together what I could from the past events and our best bet is to replicate all the preparations closely." She sets the tea down again to retrieve a tablet from her massive purse that occupies the seat next to her. "Bonus points, if we can add something to stand apart from the others."

We talk for a couple of hours to plan through the event as best we can. At some point I order us sandwiches from the kitchen and the cherry pie from the display case that they are so well known for.

"Are you okay?" she asks me when I've gone quiet for a little too long. The conversation trailed off, but suddenly, the sandwich I ordered isn't very appealing. Her question is genuine despite me not earning any concern from her.

"I'm—" The urge to lie is strong. I consider doing it but when I meet the green of her eyes, I respond honestly. "I'm barely hanging on. I've been thinking about my Mom a lot recently."

Maybe it's the nostalgia of the pie or the surprisingly soothing nature of Zadie's voice that makes me feel like sharing something that I haven't with anyone else.

"That makes sense. She was a special woman," she nods. "She was your mother. It'd be hard to forget her even if you weren't close."

I've been carrying a truth for so long that is weighing on my soul more and more each day. I don't know what possesses me to say something, but I do. "I haven't talked to my family about this at all yet. I'm sure that any of them could speculate at this point, but I've been trying to deal with it on my own. The last time that all of this came up, it didn't end well."

Her glittering eyes focus on my face in a way that I can feel, increasing the vulnerability of the moment. She speaks slowly and deliberately. "The last time? What last time?"

Inhaling deeply, I admit, "Around Christmas time last year my sister told me that she found something that was hidden away in Mom's office." For some reason, my throat has gotten thick with emotion as I think over that time where my life had truly hit rock-bottom—emotionally anyway. "I was already dealing with what I thought was too much for one man to handle-losing a parent." But then seeing that ID... I shake my head twice. "Korra found this ID from a man who looks almost identical to me. It was wrapped up in Mom's office. I had no idea why I never knew it was."

She sits with my words for a moment, processing what I've said. "Well, who was he and how did he look like you?"

The little cafe is peaceful though there are more people here than just us. I can hardly hear them from the increasing speed of my heart as I blurt all of this out to Zadie. "I can't be certain... But I'm pretty positive that he is my birth-father. There's no way that this man is not my father." I run a hand over my face and then pull at my beard and frustration. "Every time I look in the mirror, it's more and more obvious that this man had to be my birth-father. To make everything worse, Kasey found a journal that had another picture of a much younger version of my Mom in this man together. She must've been in high school or something I don't know. But what I do know is that I look nothing like Wayne Thomas. And Aiden Kendrick looks exactly like me. The only difference is likely our skin tones. It's hard to tell because the photo is in black-and-white. All the photos were in black-and-white. One from a news article and the other from the ID.

"Then the twins found a video of him and Mom singing together and it haunts me. I've started unknowingly playing the song whenever I sit down with my piano. It's bizarre and I can't take how unsure all of this makes me. I don't know anyone who knew this man. And on top of everything, Dad's been giving me a hard time as I've been trying to manage all of this in my mind." I'm damn near wheezing when I'm done dumping the contents of my mind onto the table between us. If she were to get up and go right now, I wouldn't blame her. It's none of her responsibility to do anything with the trauma I've laid at her feet.

"Wow," she breathes. "That is..." Reaching into her purse, she pulls out a large hair clip and puts her hair into some sort of twist on top of her head. "What about your siblings? Don't they know? You should be able to talk to them about it. Right?"

"You would think," I huff out a laugh that is devoid of any authentic humor. "They basically told me to bury it because they don't want to upset Wayne right now. Since he's been doing so well, recovering, and healing from the loss of our Mom and his wife."

Zadie appears even more perplexed by my response. "That can't be right. That's not how you all are. Y'all have always been super close. Everybody has each other's backs…" Her words trails off as her attention moves from her hands to my face showing all the proof that the words I'm saying are true.

"Yea, everybody does have each other's backs. But it's always for the greater good of the family. And the truth, that we all can acknowledge is right there in front of us, would not be for the greater good of the family. After losing our Mom, the next worst thing would be breaking our Dad by exposing what was truly there."

She nods her head, shifting in the cafe chair before recrossing her legs. "There has to be more to this than what you think it is. I know your siblings don't want you to talk to Wayne about it, but there has to be something that can be middle ground. You can get the answers that you need about your real parents while still being able to support your family."

"Well, that's the thing. That's the big glaring, obviously messy, thing that's standing in between me and my family right now. Nobody wants to acknowledge that. There is some sort of unrest here. I'm not the only person that can acknowledge that this is a situation that could blow everything up. But I have to hold onto it. I don't want to upset my Dad. Even if he's not my biological father, he is the man who raised me.

"Throughout my life, I felt like such an outsider and my Mom was the one who really made me feel like I belonged. My Dad was there to encourage me, as well, but I can't help thinking about the fact that both of them had lied to me. I know Wayne did not see me and think that I was his. Everybody else looks just like him and Mom. I'm the only one that doesn't. Genetics can be weird—I know that. But this was definitely a big secret that they both kept from me.

"And my siblings are fine to just bury it under the rug because it's not affecting everything that they know about themselves as much as it's affecting me. I call myself the *good guy* by listening to their advice—by not going to Wayne and demanding to know what was going on here. But what if I did go to him and he's blindsided? He may not know *anything*. Can I deal with being the person who broke the perfect image that he has of his wife?"

When I finish my word vomit, Zadie blows out an even longer exhale than the first. Her shoulders drooping with the weight of my words. "It's not fair to anybody for you to keep this as a secret. *It's eating you up.* And though he may not like it, the truth is the truth, no matter when it comes out. And it's always better for it to come out sooner rather than later."

"I'm not ready to become an orphan. I already lost my Mom. I can't lose my Dad anymore than I already have as I try to bury what's on my heart. I definitely can't lose my siblings as I try to figure out who I am when I'm not fully a part of the family anymore."

"You are still a part of the family," she says, but I can't accept that. *Not from her.*

"It's not the same."

"I know what that's like," Zadie says, reaching for my hand.

Pulling my hand from underneath hers, I reject her assumption entirely. The offense I feel from her words is a tangible snarl on my face. "How could you say that? You don't know anything about what *this* is like."

"Oh," she responds, eyes growing colder as she continues, "I don't know about being the odd one out? I'm one of the only biracial kids in this town, let alone the only one with natural red hair and green eyes. I never fit in anywhere including either side of my family. Not for lack of trying on their or my part. Me? The polyglot who traveled the world, where she was the only person who looked like her in every country she visited, to come back and still things are the same. On top of the fact that I am being persecuted by my nepo baby coworker because he feels that things aren't one-to-one on who has had life the hardest. I know exactly what it's like to not belong where you should, especially in family, but also in life. You trauma dumped all over me, having all these existential-crisis ass problems, then you're upset when I try to relate to you?" She stands, gathering her things and putting them into her bag. "You're having a hard time and there's much on your plate that would be upsetting for anyone. But maybe when you go to ask someone for advice, don't do whatever the hell that just was." With that, she leaves me sitting with the pies we purchased and the bitter taste of unrest on my tongue.

Her words sting even though they are true. I don't chase her out of the cafe because I don't know how to respond to her words. I've made myself look like a complete ass. Not just look—I was a complete ass.

When did I become this terrible at communicating like a regular human being?

Why is it always Zadie that brings this out of me?

Why is she calling me a spoiled nepo baby?

I roll my eyes and run a hand over my hair. *It's obvious as to why.* I've been acting that way and leave it to Zadie to read me better than anyone else can.

Chapter 18

Lee

"Well, the case I'm working on right now involves the Brenfords doing their best to work against a new restaurant opening in town," Bryce says from the couch in his house. A rather large fern frond brushes his arm, but he seems unbothered by the excess of greenery trailing around him. Somewhere in the house, their kitten is playing vigorously with a toy that tinkles every now and again. The sound of her bouncing off of surfaces to capture it should be adorable, but I'm not able to enjoy it. The awkward tension in the room from Bryce's words puts me on edge.

The last time I was at my sister's new house, I bolted out of here. Though we haven't talked about it I know that everyone in this room, including my little sister, knows about it. My siblings have been walking on eggshells around me and it's uncomfortable for us all.

I try to relax in the chair I've chosen by the door, but there are so many people in the house that it makes it a little difficult to focus on anyone in particular. "Why would they not want a restaurant to open up?" I ask.

"A very good question," he says. "But after some digging it seems that the owner of the restaurant is a family member who has led the charge of all the fallout the Brenfords are still experiencing now."

"Who is it?" Zach asks, looking like he's moments from falling asleep in the overstuffed recliner closest to the dining room.

"Shepard Kindrick. He's trying to open a new-style American spot," Bryce says plainly. "Supposedly, he's got a good reputation from all we could find. Wynn suggested I lead this one and it's been very frustrating. The Brenfords sit on every board. But with the continuous push back on community events that seem to earn them favor with others in Harmony Hill, it's going to be a close call if they are going to make it happen."

Wynn West owns the law firm in town that has made it their mission to protect the citizens of Harmony Hill from increasing misgivings from the Brenford family. They own the steel mill that employs many people in this town—at one point, my birth-father too. Their favor in this way has run its course with more and more lawsuits coming up than they can squash with their funds alone.

For several years, Bryce had worked for a much larger law firm in Denver until he got serious about my big sister. Somehow, Wynn, and likely Korra, convinced him to leave the big leagues to fight for the little guys here. It's admirable, sure, but I only believed there to be petty feuds that they were fighting. With someone so close to home giving insight on what has been going on, it's clear that the Brenfords have very little concern for their community.

"Kindrick?" Korra asks, looking towards Kasey. They share a look that communicates what I think it does.

"Yea. Spelled the same and all," Bryce confirms.

Everyone looks toward me.

At some point I had stopped breathing.

It seems that I won't get any peace walking into Korra's house. Each time, a new ticking bomb is placed in my lap.

It never occurred to me that there would be someone else who maybe knew my dead birth-father. This person shares the same last name, it's likely that they could have known Aiden.

Whoever they are, they're stirring up shit with the Brenfords. A ballsy move and an ill-advised one.

I shake my head to clear it before I ask, "What reason would the Brenfords have in blocking him opening a restaurant?"

Bryce looks down to Korra who sits beside him. "Well, for starters, the Kindrick family used to be a powerhouse in this town. They moved on after a huge falling out with the Brenfords. And I suspect that they are the driving force behind all of the negative press that's been coming up. It's not been confirmed, but with how hard their lawyers are fighting against them it would seem that's the case."

Zach pipes up, pressing the button to sit up in the reclining chair. "What do you mean they were a powerhouse? For as long as I've known, the Brenfords have run everything."

"It wasn't always like that," Bryce clarifies. "It was two families that had foundations in this town. The Kindricks and the Brenfords. But if Shepherd is able to get clearance to open up this business, then that will just be one route, of likely many more routes, to come after what opening is being left from the Brenfords.

Somehow finding the energy, Zach proposes a good point. "If the Kindricks are truly going after the Brenfords, then shouldn't we want them to take their place? The Brenfords are always at the forefront of some malicious actions that get covered up with a new event or something else. They're too far tied to truly go away."

Kasey counters his point with arms and legs crossed, a severe ponytail swishing with her words. "If the Kindricks were once at the same level as them, then shouldn't we be wary of them as well?"

Bryce shakes his head. "I don't think it's that simple. But I do know that there is no legal reason why Shepherd shouldn't be able to open his business. He did everything that he needed to do. The only reason why he's not able to open up this establishment is because of the pushback from one family's interest. And if that interest solely lies with the fact that they don't want the Kindricks to have a better withstanding in the community, then I'm siding with the Kindricks. Wynn thinks so and I'm on his side in this."

Curiosity has risen in me as I don't truly know what could come from having someone who is from the Kindrick family in town. I have so many questions to ask. The biggest one is—did he know my birth-father?

But an easy follow up would be—who is he to Aiden?

There's a sickness roiling in my gut at the thought that the Brenfords have something to do with the reason why Aiden is no longer with us.

Clearing my throat to push the sickness back, I say, "Listen up, there is something that we all need to get on the same page about."

"Oh, yes. I did want to ask about that too," Korra says. "We're doing a winter-slash-Valentine's spread for the scrapbook. I'd really love more hands to complete it. These projects are really more fun with others—"

"No," I say. "That is not what I'm talking about. That competition is closed anyway as the Brenfords swim through all their legal troubles. Not a priority."

"So what is it?" Zach asks, cautious in his tone.

It's likely because I feel sick to my stomach at having to bring this up, but I can't keep holding this on my shoulders alone. Despite everything, I need my family. I can't keep holding everything close to my chest or I will explode.

I already have.

With a deep inhale in to find the calm, so my words don't come out wavering, I inform them of the news I've been keeping a secret. "Wayne Thomas is not my birth-father."

The words drop like a bomb in the room. At one point booming in my ears then the silence of the destruction coming at once.

Too many responses all come at once for me to discern what is being said. "Not everyone at once," Zach says. "Let's start with the most important question. How do you know this for certain?"

Facing him, I say, "I got my birth certificate. I had never looked it over before. Mom always submitted that kind of paperwork and then I had a passport or drivers license. I never paid it any attention. There is no name on the document where the father's name should be."

“That doesn’t mean anything,” Bryce chimes in. “It could always be amended.”

“And it never was. I found the other birth certificates in Mom’s room and everyone else has one, including Nia. But I don’t. Why would she do that if not for a reason?”

“Because having five kids is a lot of work, sometimes things get lost in the busyness of that,” Kasey says. “I thought we squashed this already.”

“Look, whether you all believe it or not, Wayne is not my birth-father. I won’t know until we take a DNA test. But this man, Aiden, is more likely to be my father than you all realize.”

“A DNA test?” Korra asks with wide eyes. “You’re going to ask our Dad for a DNA test? Why do you need that?”

I thought that telling them might alleviate some of the weight, but it makes me feel like I’m on display for the pain I’ve been dealing with. In having to defend what I want as well as hold firm to what I know to be true. “How else will I know for sure?”

Kasey leans forward on the couch. “You could get a test with this Aiden guy. It can’t be that hard to track him down.”

I tilt my head to the side as my siblings wait for my response. “I could if he were alive. He died almost two months before my birth.”

The collective murmur amongst them is disheartening.

“You couldn’t have any idea of what I’m going through right now. Everything I knew about my family is not even built on a solid truth of my mother and father. Mom lied to me for my whole life. *So did Dad.* Every day they had the opportunity to tell me the truth and no one ever did. I won’t even know why. I’ll never be able to ask Mom why she felt it was so important to hide Aiden from me. If I left it in your hands then I’d have to wonder if Wayne ever knew or not.” Zadie’s own sentiments for the matter ring in my mind, coming out as my own thoughts. “Isn’t the truth always better than a lie?”

Korra reaches across the coffee table to hold my hand. “Is it?” Her eyes are earnest.

She truly wants to know, I have no answers for her.

Is knowing all that I already discovered better now that it has come to light?

No.

It fucking sucks to have the rug ripped from under you. There is no worse feeling than that. I swear that ever since she found that ID, my world has felt more and more unstable.

I can't answer her question in the way that I want to. I don't know what I could say so I don't reply, letting her hand linger on mine like I now wish I'd let Zadie's.

Zach breaks the tense silence when I don't open my mouth to answer Korra's question. "So, what do you want us to do about it?"

This is what has been destroying me the most.

When we all found out about the ID, there was no support for my point of view. They jumped to protect Wayne instead of considering me. I honestly can see why that would be the first gut reaction. Over the past year, we all have been trying to mediate between the hurts of our collective loss and anything that could instigate it further.

As a family, that is what we're meant to do. We're meant to protect each other.

But their instinct to protect boxed me out. Intentionally or unintentionally.

"I want you all to be on my side. To see things from my perspective and back me up. This one instance, I need you to put yourself in my shoes and see how much I need this."

"What do you need?" Kasey asks, genuinely focused on me, listening intently to my next words.

"I'm going to tell Dad what I know. I'm going to ask him for a paternity test."

Korra stands, breaking the hold her fiancé has on her shoulders. "I'll go with you, Lee. If this is something that you need for your peace of mind then you can count me in."

"We should call Nia. She deserves to know what the family is deciding," Zach says with his phone already pressed to his ear.

My baby sister picks up and I feel like a jerk for not telling her about what's been going on with me. I didn't know how or when I would tell her about *my news*. I'll just have to add it to my never-ending list of shortcomings at this point.

Zach tells her the root of his call in succinct points that I can hear Nia gasp over, even when she isn't on speakerphone. After a bit of their broken back-and-forth, Zach places the phone on the coffee table and presses the speaker button.

The first thing my sister says through the crackle of the phone is, "I'm so sorry, big bro. I hope you know I'd be squeezing you so hard right now. If I weren't preparing my thesis, I'd be on the first bus home."

"That's not necessary. You focus on your books so you can walk across that stage. You'll be done before you know it and you can hug me then."

Kasey interrupts, "As touching as this is, we need to know your opinion on the matter at hand."

"Isn't it obvious? I'll stand beside Lee for whatever he decides to do. I'm shocked to hear that Mom was creeping on Dad, but Lee deserves to know who his birth-father is... Even if it does turn out to be Dad."

Zach picks his phone up. "It's settled then. We'll all go together to have this talk with Dad. It's going to be hard but with you and Zadie putting this adoption on, we should probably wait until after then. Is that too long?"

"It's not. I've waited my whole life. What's another couple weeks in the grand scheme of things?"

Chapter 19

Lee

It feels strange to knock on the door that I usually walk right into. Yet, here I am knocking.

I've had a key to my sisters' flat since they got locked out in the first few months that they lived here. When Zadie moved in and Korra moved out, they never changed the locks. Outside the front door, the planters still look familiar, but I know the inside of this place looks completely different now that Korra has taken her plant babies with her. Most of the signature plants were assaulting Bryce at their place yesterday.

I don't actually know what this flat looks like now. There is no information I have to make an assumption about it either.

I rock back and forth on my heels waiting for either of the women to answer the front door. Several minutes pass where no one does and I knock again.

There is no response, but instead my phone vibrates in my pocket. I pick up and it's Zadie's sleepy voice on the other end. "Why are you at my door, uninvited?"

"Were you sleeping?" is all I can think of to respond. It's a mixture of the sexy quality of the rasp in her deeper voice and the thought now of what she sleeps in that distracts my purpose in coming here.

"It's my off-day. Of course, I'm sleeping." She yawns and adds, "Well, not anymore since I had to go see who exactly is knocking at my door uninvited."

We'd spent the last week vaccinating and prepping countless animals that are going up for adoption next week. It didn't feel like much time had passed since we'd come to the agreement to work together. I regret how within this week we'd been even more distant with each other than before she'd agree to work at Thomas & Friends. It was my fault since I acted like a complete ass at the café the weekend prior. My highest priority is to make that right. Even if my thoughts are taking me in a different direction entirely.

"Yes, I was uninvited," I confirm, but with no sound of her unlocking the door I ask, "Can I come in?"

"Depends," is all she says.

When she doesn't elaborate, I'm forced to question what these stipulations are. Whatever it is, I'll have to comply. Though we go back-and-forth often, I don't suspect that she would ever make me suffer for my misgivings. It's just another way that she is better than me. "On what?"

I can hear her voice from the other side of the door as well as on my phone now. "Whether I feel like getting my head chewed off for being a decent human being."

Shit.

"I came to apologize about that. I—Please let me in. I really don't want to apologize to the door." I don't add, *though I will if I have to.*

"Fine," she says. A few moments later, the safety latch and door click before she appears.

"When did you get a security latch?" I ask before I truly get a look at Zadie standing there.

Her red curls are piled on top of her head with a blush scarf that matches the pajamas she's wearing. *Pajamas* might not be the correct term for how little the clothes are on her body. A thin pink camisole hangs from one shoulder with the thin strap dangling over her tattoo. The matching silky shorts are lost in her plush thighs, exposing the smallest hint to the curve of her ass.

So much of her skin is on display and it's messing with my head even more than her throaty voice.

"Your sisters never had one. I got one installed by the landlord. There is no way I'm living in a place on my own without one."

"Huh?" I respond, lost in the tantalizing sway of her hips as she walks toward her bedroom.

She turns to face me in the hall in front of her door. I stop walking in time to not bump right into her when she says, "The security latch. I got it—Bent, eyes up here."

I snap my jaw shut, meeting her eyes. "I'm sorry. I just... Do you have a robe or something?" I don't bother to correct her calling me *Bent*. I'm too embarrassed by my own actions since I'm already coming to her to apologize for how I was a dick to her the other day. She was genuinely trying to help me, but I was too sensitive to see that. Even in her upset, she was able to give me perspective that I desperately needed. Here I am checking her out because I'm an idiot who can't stop fucking up around her.

Her eyes narrow. "No, I do not. You came here, uninvited—I cannot stress that part enough—so get to the point of you coming here before I kick you out."

Looking down the other hall to see if my sister's home, I determine she's not since the bedroom light isn't on. "Can we sit for a bit?" I ask, nodding over towards the couch in the living room.

"Sure," she says, but doesn't walk to the shared area. Instead she opens her bedroom door and walks toward her bed.

It amazes me just how large this bedroom is without all the greenery that once was. While she gets comfortable in her sheets, I take a seat on the vanity chair I've pulled out from the dressing table she has in the left corner. A massive TV is mounted on the wall across from her bed that is all being framed by endless albums and merchandise from PFP. While I'm not one to collect physical albums, I've seen these covers on my streaming app and their futuristic merch is unmistakable.

In between posters and plushies are countless photos of Zadie in places she's visited and even more of sights I've never seen. In several photos, she's holding animals from her travels. In others, she's simply posing with strangers I don't know. Some are in unique frames of their own and others are simply pinned with decorative push pins. It's impressive to say the very least. She's got this view every time she sits in her bed.

She clears her throat to bring my attention back to her. "You were apologizing..." she prompts.

"Oh, right." *I'm here for a reason.* It's not just some random visit. Sitting up a little taller on the padded bench seat, I begin, "It was out of line for me to go off on you like that at the café. I was feeling sensitive because of the memories and all the drama, but none of that is your fault or your burden. Learning to control my worst thoughts has to be a skill that I improve on my own. We got good work done and I truly believe that if we're on the same page, this adoption event will be successful. I'm sorry that you had to deal with my shitty attitude when you were only trying to relate. I'm sorry. I'll try to do better."

Zadie doesn't respond right away. She lets my apology linger in the room as I fight the urge to fidget under her gaze.

"Mmh," she hums after a few moments have passed in our silence. "I-Is this groveling? It is pretty delicious."

I rub a hand down my face. "Must you—"

"Oh. I must," she nods with emphasis, making her curls bounce on the top of her head. "There is something especially delicious about this particular flavor of you on your knees."

On my knees? "What do you mean?"

"If I so decide, I could return the favor and kick you out of the event at this point. I've gotten everything organized. I even have heard back from the volunteers…"

"Zadie," I start but don't know where to go with that statement. With everything that has happened, it would serve her right to leave me off of the event's information and let my Dad think that I didn't do anything to contribute.

Her smirk is downright sinister as she relents, "I won't, but I very well could. I thought about it long and hard because I was beyond pissed leaving the café. You're lucky that I'm an evolved person. Besides, you've been dealt a shit hand without my input anyway."

A breath of relief rushes from me and I lean over with my head in my hands.

If she wanted, she could demolish my chances in one move. It would be easy.

This way we could still be in this together. Unlike our everyday work in the clinic, an event at this scale would be a nightmare to be in charge of alone. In as short a time frame as we've been given, I don't want to leave anything to chance that she has to handle on her own.

Shaking her head, she chuckles. "Just wait 'til I tell the twins about you coming here."

"You told my sisters about what happened?" Heat crawls up my neck at the thought.

She studies her nails as she replies flippantly. "Well heaven forbid I report back to headquarters. It's called peer review."

I squint at her. "It feels reductive that you're trying to use language to relate to me as a man."

"Did it work?" She laughs her throaty laugh. "You're so uptight, Bent. Please relax. I didn't give your sisters a play by play of anything. Not Christmas and certainly not you losing your shit at the café. I'm doing my best to forget about it for both our sakes."

"Why would you want to forget?" Obviously, I meant Christmas. It would be to both of our benefits for her to forget what happened last weekend.

Her expression is genuinely puzzled with my words. "Why would I want to forget?" She blinks a few times. "Is that a serious question?"

I nod. "Why wouldn't it be?"

With a tilt to her head, a few of her curls spring out of the hair scarf. "Because you've tortured me with the memory over my head for the past few months."

"Tortured is a bit much." I didn't realize I had talked about it that much. But seeing as it was clearly a pain point of hers, I imagine that taking advantage of that one area of weakness would be used... often enough. Or more aptly, it's been on my mind enough that it's come out of my mouth just as often.

"Is it?" Her blanket falls from her shoulders as she sits up on the bed. "And I quote, '*Was it the cider that had you moaning or was it me?*' All your little digs you get in." She shakes her head. "We had sex. Yes, I enjoyed it." Then she stands up from the bed, kicking her blanket off of her as she goes. "From the sound of it, I wasn't the only one."

"You're right. I did enjoy it," I throw my hands up in the air, crossing the room and standing close to her. "In fact, I can't stop thinking about it. All the damn time, the thought of you and me and that night assaults me. Every time I see you all I can think of is how soft your skin is, how good you feel, how right you taste. But what good does that do me?" The smell of her hair brings the memories into full focus as I'm within her vicinity again.

Zadie looks up at me with wide eyes that somehow manage to sparkle even covered by the shadow of my body.

I don't know what I was going to do before I came over here.

All of that is out of the window.

The way her pupils widen, making the green nearly disappear, as she looks at me is more than I can take.

My hands tremble when I put them on her waist.

She doesn't hesitate to put hers around my neck.

Leaning my head down, she meets me halfway in a kiss that feels like there will be more that follows. It's a comma rather than an exclamation point while my heart races in my chest.

I need her to want this because I don't think I can stop.

I didn't come here for this.

I never thought that I would feel her pillow soft lips pressing against mine, but then again you can't plan for dreams like this one to come true.

You have to fall and hope that your demise isn't on the other side.

There is only one reason why this woman hasn't left my mind since that one night, and frankly, has always been in my thoughts. It's clear that our connection is undeniable despite how I have been denying it.

Try as hard as I might, I want the woman who can show me more. Who dares to reach for what she wants regardless of what obstacles might stand in her way.

I admire her.

Breaking our kiss, I look over the face that has been the fuel for my own betterment for nearly a lifetime. Those lips, swollen and kiss bitten. Her eyes, half-mast, but still bright under curly dark-brown lashes. Every sweet freckle scattered over her face...

Zadie has been my reason.

She's why I proved myself and felt pride when I accomplished these things in my life that felt insurmountable. Even now, she's pushed me to face everything that I've been hiding under callous words and a bad attitude.

In this moment, all I want is to prove to her that what happened on Christmas between us was the best thing that could have ever happened to me.

Taking her lips again, I deepen our kiss. Slipping my tongue inside, I bring her flush against my body. I need to feel her softness embracing against my hardness.

Her soft moan is loud in the otherwise quiet room as my thigh presses between her legs. She uses me for only a moment before I walk her back to the bed. When her thighs meet the side of the mattress, I lift her easily onto the edge.

"You just picked me up like I weigh nothing," she pants as I kneel on the carpet. Her amused gaze follows me down with her arms still around my neck. She unclasps her hands to run her fingers through my beard and up into my hair.

"I don't go to the gym for no reason," I say between soft skin that's begging for my marks.

She chuckles and falls back onto the bed. Thick thighs rise in the air with her fall. I take the opportunity to catch them onto my shoulders, placing me right where I want to be.

She gasps, leaning up on her elbows. "What are you doing?" She asks, but it's clear where I'm going next.

I ask anyway so that I'm able to do what I have been hoping for. "Can I pull these little shorts to the side so that I can plunge my tongue deep inside of you?"

Chapter 20

Zadie

"Can I pull these little shorts to the side so that I can plunge my tongue deep inside of you?"

How did I get here?

Heat floods my face for only a moment before my core tightens with realization.

Bentley is going to devour me.

His intensity could be something that powers whole homes as he waits so patiently on his knees in front of me.

I had only joked before about how good he looks groveling. But… "Show me that you deserve to taste me again," I say with a brow lifted.

That intensity flickers for only a moment before he kisses just above my thigh. It's so soft that I barely feel his mouth. Shivers roll down my spine, but I don't dare move. I want to see what he will do next.

He trails several more kisses up my thigh. By the time he gets halfway to my core, my toes are curling. The mix of his full lips and soft beard teasing me is sending me over the edge. Every ounce of stretch and determination is going into keeping my thighs apart for him to continue doing what he's doing.

"Tell me that you're sorry for how you acted again," I pant in the breathiest voice I've ever heard from myself.

Between kisses, he says, "I'm– so– sorry– please– let– me– show– you– how– much–"

My eyes roll back now that he is only a centimeter from my thigh crease. Shit. I'm not going to be able to hold off any more. Combining his desperate words with the grip he has on my hips and his soft mouth has been a revelation in self control.

But I wasn't wrong—Bentley looks damn good on his knees.

"You've earned it," I say, waiting for him to meet my eye again. When he does, I know I'm in for it.

Quicker than I could have expected, he pulls my sleep shorts off. The blush silk fabric slinking down off the bed. I don't bother leaving the camisole on, choosing to pull it over my hair.

Still on my elbows, I've got an amazing view of Bentley's flat tongue running up and over my lips to my clit before he swirls it over the tip of my sensitive bud. A jolt of pleasure, hot and sticky, rolls down my spine as he continues circling it with just the tip of his tongue.

"Shit, I miss that," I cry out, head rolling back down between my shoulders. "You know just how much."

"I figured," he says, licking two thick fingers to tease them at my entrance. I'm dripping and the sound of him playing with me is messy and loud in my room. With just the first knuckles teasing into me, I'm clenching against nothing. "How about this?" He asks, mischief on his lips that still glisten with me.

"Oh, you know–" I interrupt my own words with a gasp when he slides them in deeper and twists to press up inside me. "Bentley," I cry out.

"I love how my name sounds on your desperate breaths," he gloats, going harder and more intentionally with his fingers. "Is it because I'm spelling it out in this tight pussy?"

My eyes roll and I'm unable to respond. We both know that I agree. We know it because my legs are now clenching his hand in place as an orgasm unexpectedly rolls over me in harsh shudders I can't control.

"That's it, red. Give me more," Bentley coos.

As I finally come down from the high, I open my eyes to Bentley still there in front of me, but this time he's not focused on me. He's palming himself over his sweats.

He's waiting.

He's waiting for me to tell him what he can do next.

I smirk, asking, "Would you like to come, Bentley?"

He nods repeatedly, doing his best to remove the pants without getting off his knees.

This is doing something to me.

It's doing something for me.

I am into this—very much so.

As he rights himself back into a kneeling position, I demand, "Shirt off."

He rips it off of himself and tosses it somewhere in the room. On display this way, I get an unobstructed view of his sculpted body and stiff erection that bobs up near his belly button. He doesn't touch himself though he could, he looks hard enough that it should hurt. A dribble of precum sliding down his length in a show of wanting.

Licking my lips, I curl my finger toward me.

I need him on me.

Taking himself in hand, he crawls onto the bed between my legs. I like the focus in his eyes as we both crawl backward. I can't stop myself from reaching for him again.

He's hard and heated in my hands as I stroke him. His hand covers mine as we stroke his length together, our eyes never leaving the others. My grip tightens over the crown of him, my thumb whispering over his slit.

"Zadie," he breathes against my neck. It's pained and the first time that we've broken eye contact since we started.

I feel the loss of his gaze and I want it back.

Holding his jaw, I move his head to look at me again. "I'm here, Bentley." His eyes flick between mine before I repeat, "I'm here."

He kisses me again. The taste of me is on our tongues clashing, but the warmth of this connection is stronger than I could have imagined.

The beginning of all this is unclear. I don't know and I don't care how we ended up like this. With me settling myself over him, arms wrapped around his neck and him supporting me as we grind together.

I didn't even think about what this could mean moving forward. I just knew that he feels good inside me and our bodies feel good when they come together like this.

Surrendering to this force that's pulling us together is better—so much better—the second time around, especially with us sober for it.

We lie on my bed, both of us exhausted from the emotional and physical toll of what just happened between us.

I never thought that I would end up in bed with him again, but I'm not upset by this turn of events. Being Lee's enemy was not my goal.

It never has been.

I just wanted him to respect the truth of our circumstances.

"Why are you so determined to get this role at the clinic?" I roll over onto my side so that I can fully face him. "In your position, I'd just go somewhere else. Somewhere that didn't come with all—" I gesture to the space between us, hoping that my meaning is clear, "this. I would never stand for what your Dad is doing right now."

"At first, it was simply because it had always been my goal post. I knew that I wanted to be where he is in life. Get married, have my own practice, have kids. But over time I realized that there were things that were too different between us—from him and I—that I just couldn't let go of. Then when I saw that we really weren't related, it hit me like a ton of bricks.

"It doesn't matter how hard I work or what I'm going through. He doesn't believe that I'm cut out to replace him. There never should have been a hiring process. He had someone to take over for him all along. He still hired you. He still favors you. Better than me or not, I was never good enough."

The pain in his eyes is palpable from here. I wish that I could do something to make that pain go away.

This competition between us is not fun when all these elements are clear to me. I don't know what to say. My mouth is dry and words escape me when I reach for any sort of response.

That doesn't deter Bentley from letting more of his pain out into the space between us. He huffs an unamused sound. "For my entire life, Mom hid the truth from me. I'll never know why or to what end because she's gone. I've been parsing through every memory we had together to try and find some point where she might have slipped and told me something that I couldn't understand at that moment. Like she maybe left me a hint that I wouldn't grasp at that age, but I could now... There's nothing."

He twists the sheet underneath him, "I may not be the brightest of sunshine rays, but I do have feelings. The man she left me with would see fit to replace me than to ask about what is going on. There is zero curiosity at why I've not been on my game, why I've been distracted. He hasn't asked me once about my breakup. He hasn't even questioned why I've been upset with him."

"You don't have to be blood relatives for you to be family," I say though his eyes are already defiant behind slightly smudged glasses. "You don't even have to do everything he's done in his life to be a good son. It's possible for you to strike your own path and still be a good son. He may be going through his own things as well. He lost his partner in life and I imagine it will take a long time to recover from that."

"It's not just that. It's actually so much more than that, he shakes his head. "Belonging is thick in my memories. In my family, everyone had a role and a place. Korra is the sensitive one. Kasey is the clever one. Zach is the compassionate one. Nia is the sweet one. But I was their favorite for a time. It wasn't set in stone but I *had favor*. Mom spent the most time with me and the music. My dad showed me everything he could about his clinic. I have memories of us being happy. Both of them, all of us. But there was something underneath which kept me at some distance." He leans his head back onto the headboard. "It was probably made up. I was just spoiled or some shit. But in photos, when I look back there is someone who sticks out and that someone is me."

The thought is strong in my mind and I quickly bat it away when I remember the last time I tried relating to him. Things are different now, they must be, but I'm still nervous when I say, "You don't want to hear it, but I know how that feels. Truly. Your memories will always be yours. You can look back on them fondly and savor the happiness. Or, you can look back and only pick at the snags and flaws in them. The choice is yours on how you spend your reverie. All we have are our memories to tell us about how we've spent our time on this planet. I'd rather spend mine recounting the happiness of those moments. I've worked hard to make them so."

He's quiet for a moment. He's actually quiet so long that I think he might have gone to sleep when he rolls over to face me in the bed, propping his head up on his fist. "You're right."

I take a chance on grabbing his hand, to support him—to reconnect.

He surprises me by intertwining our fingers.

We lie there for a few more moments, enjoying this reprieve.

Then he sighs, "I just don't know what to do. I talked to my siblings, but trying to decide on what my next step isn't any easier."

It's good that he finally talked to them. We both know that's not good enough for his circumstances. "You should tell him what you know. He deserves to know the truth."

I see his beard twitch with how he grinds his teeth in discomfort. "It's no more appealing now than it was when you suggested it the first time."

"You'll never get the answers you're looking for if you don't."

He rolls over to cage me in the strength of his arms. His shoulders and chest flexing in my line of sight. "There is only one answer I'm looking for right now."

I raise an eyebrow at him. "What answer is that?"

"Are we going to have sex again?" With a smile that belies his turmoil, he adds, "I'd really like to."

I should have said no.

In hindsight, I know that I should have. But I honestly can't resist a pliant and willing Bentley Thomas.

More than that, I've made up my mind.

If he doesn't have the strength to do it. Then, I can do it for him.

Chapter 21

Lee

The engine hums beneath me as I wait for Zadie to finally come out of the apartment. Ever since she and I had it out, I've been hooked. I couldn't tell you exactly what changed, but all I know is that I can't waste any more time fighting the pull that I have toward her.

The sun is out, making the weather feel less harsh than it is with February coming to a close and March strong on the horizon. Just before the rains and sleet showers kick up again, it's perfect conditions for a cool drive. People usually prefer to ride when the weather is warm. I do love a good summer ride too. But there is something about the cool air and sleepy landscape that appeals to me. I can't resist it.

"Hey," she calls from the final step before hoisting a backpack onto her shoulders.

"What's in the bag?" I ask since this isn't her typical massive handbag. I've never seen it before and it bulges from how it's stuffed full.

Zadie saunters over to where I've parked. She grabs the helmet that I'm holding out for her. Today, she has her bright red curls braided down into one thick braid that makes her look a little more fierce than I've ever seen her. In a heavy duty jacket and boots, she makes a sight that I know will not leave my brain anytime soon. I bet she'd make for a sexy grid girl. I'd love to see her in an outfit that suits my ride or better yet, without any of that and just her draped naked over my bike...

I push those thoughts away when she says, "You'll see," in answer to my earlier question.

She then climbs onto the back of my bike and tucks her arms around my waist. Her soft fingers slide under my jacket to touch my skin. I shiver though her hands are warm. Who knew that she would fit here like she's done this a hundred times. Like maybe we've been this easy and everything is how it should be.

"Don't take it easy on me," she says, leaning over my shoulder. "I like the curves."

"Me, too," I tell her, not talking about the road at all.

Laughing to myself, I ease us out and down the county road that leads to the one highway up the Hills. Just before the elevation increases, their view is incredible. The wide expanse of hill tops rolling into one another are a revelation when the sky is clear like it is today. The golden grass and big blue sky are unmissable. We pass the few weathered fences that keep horses, cows and sheep contained just before the road narrows to only one view—upward.

Zadie's husky laugh is just barely audible over the wind whipping by us when I lean into the first curve around the hill. On the other side is a reservoir that isn't as high as it usually is with the winter coming to an end. The houses that are situated around and dotting up the side lie dormant since it's not the season for tourists. In summer, there are countless boats, canoes and paddle boards floating along. But this time of year the deep blue-green is still except for the occasional ripple of the wind over the surface or group of Canada geese floating by.

A settled sort of relief falls over me as Zadie holds onto me tighter around the next bend. There is something in my chest that finally loosens, when we pull off to an overlook that isn't as popular. There is no sign for it and it's not well groomed like the named ones we've passed on the way here. For a moment we stay like that, her holding me as I hold the handles of my motorcycle. When I cut the engine and silence returns, I know that I made a good choice. The sounds are the wind, distant birds and the rushing sound of water that the reservoir is processing.

After a while, Zadie swings off of the bike and takes her helmet off. I do the same then it's just us and an incredible view. I never thought that what these drives were missing was a companion to share them with. I honestly never thought to ask for one. I'd come on my own and escape everything. Now, I realize that it's much more special with someone who can understand.

"This is exactly what I miss when I'm gone," she says, spreading her arms wide as the wind floats over us. Her eyes are bright with wonder, taking in the sight before us.

I lean against the bike, watching her and the view in equal measure. "You miss it, but you still left." The words sound sharper and more accusatory than I wish they did but the emotion is confusing to me. I don't know why that is.

She shrugs, not taking offense to my words. "I needed to know what was out there. Otherwise, this," she gestures to the Hills, "doesn't feel like a choice. How can I be grateful for something, when I don't know its value?"

My throat is thick with emotion and I can't respond. She has so perfectly explained everything that I felt about losing Mom without trying. Though my emotions toward Mom are complicated, I took her for granted. I know I did and now that she's gone I'm forced to face that fact. I assumed she'd always be around and that I could *do it later* when I blew her off or missed a family event.

"I wish I had that outlook," I barely croak out.

With the emotion still thick in my voice, Zadie comes to my side. She doesn't say anything more, just sits with me and it feels good to know she's there.

After a while, we move over to a flat rock near the edge of the overlook. She gets her big backpack and starts pulling out all kinds of containers. "I did some grocery shopping," she announces proudly as I looked over all the containers.

"What is all this?" I ask, picking up one of them.

"That," she says, "is a tamarind ball. I got hooked on them in Belize." I bite into the little brown candy and my face puckers. She chuckles, throwing her head back. "They're a little bit sour and a little sweet. Kinda like you."

I drink a glug of water to wash it down. "Ha ha," I say. "Why'd you let me take such a big bite?"

Zadie leans over to kiss me. It's chaste in comparison to any we've had before but more intimate somehow.

"Nothing beats that reaction," she says with a smirk. She opens the next container after eating a bit of the tamarind ball herself. "These are fekka. Usually you'd have them with tea or coffee, but I like them on their own. They're kind of like twice-baked biscotti."

Picking up a slice, I take a smaller bite, unsure if she's going to be pranking me again. "Oh this, I like," taking a bigger bite. "Where are these from?"

"Morocco," she says, taking a bite and smiling over the taste. "I had a couple slices almost every morning when I lived there. These don't have almonds on top like the ones I had though. I've got to settle for what they have in the international section. Plus that drive to Denver to get all this stuff was not my favorite when I used to walk like seven minutes down the road to get them."

I nod, finishing my cookie. "You clearly have a sweet tooth. Did you bring anything savory or, better yet, spicy?"

"Hmm," she says, reaching into her backpack. "I've got these." I look at the package she hands me and it's actually got English writing on it beside the characters that I can't read.

"Isn't it just ramen?"

"No! Look here," she points to the corner, "Smash, don't boil."

My eyebrows shoot up. "I'm just raw-dogging some ramen noodles?"

"Hush," she says, taking the package from me. She opens it and pulls out the powder packet. Quickly, she sprinkles the seasoning inside before twisting the back closed. Using her water bottle, she smashes the package and shakes it up. "Try 'em now."

I do as she says and she was not kidding on the spicy. The flavor is good, but the spice is even higher. “I like these,” I say, holding the bag up to read the package some more.

“Good,” she says.

After trying several of her other snacks and recounting her stories about how she discovered she liked them, we ride back down the hills before the sun dips too low in the sky. Right now, everything is cast in a golden hue that brings a simple realization.

I don’t want to win this competition between us anymore.

I don't know what I’ll do instead, but I want more of this. I want to keep riding roads like this with her. I want to hear more of her stories about the places she's seen and what she did there. I want to hear her perspective on everyday things that make me see the world differently.

I don’t want to let anything get in the way of that.

How do I get from here to there though?

Chapter 22

Zadie

"I'm glad you came, princess," Mama says, while we both are balancing on one leg with the other pulled up and back. Dancer's pose is challenging, even without talking, but I feel like I'm floating. Mama comments as much, "You've found your flow again."

After weeks of returning to the practice each night and on weekends, I agree with her. Though I don't think that my diligence in taking care to connect with my body is why I'm noticeably more balanced now.

It would have to do with a certain someone not being a thorn in my side anymore.

That resolve of knowing exactly where I stand with him has given me as much peace as I think it's given him. Catching him in the hallway, getting kisses in the break room and maybe a little more... It has done wonders for aligning my mind and body.

The sun shines down on us in the sun room though I know it is more than freezing outside. We got snow last night and clumps of it still stick to the edges of the half-dome roof. "I have, haven't I? It's a nice day so that is probably helping.

Seeing genuine smiles from Bentley directed at me is another little boost of energy that I never expected to have. I look forward to seeing them, even if it's in the stolen moments that we get to have in private.

I have to be careful because Kasey Thomas is like a prime investigator when it comes to any of her siblings' love lives. Bentley ending things with his ex was all that she could talk about since her and Malaya are close. I'm not ready to put a name on what her brother and I have right now. I definitely don't need Korra to find out either with how rose-tinted her viewpoint of the world is.

"Whatever you're doing—it's working my girl." The relief in her voice makes me feel a little better as well.

I know that she worries for me when I'm away since she's never travelled farther than state lines. But I don't want her to worry when I'm home as well.

We follow through the rest of our session letting our breaths guide our movements until we both end on our mats in a seated position.

I scratch my shoulder and ask, "Mama, do you remember when Oliver would come out here because he thought it was one giant puppy relief area?"

She chuckles, "That rascal, yes. I remember him getting startled at me finding him and him getting caught up under the humidifier. Took your Daddy a while to fix that mess."

"Oh, I forgot about the humidifier! He was so curious..." My words trail off as I remember that day. "What would you think about me getting another dog?"

Mama considers me, her deep brown eyes assessing my face. After a few moments she asks, "Do you think you're ready for that?"

"I don't know. It's been on my mind for a while. I think I might be."

She reaches over to rub my hand, "You'll know when you've found that special friend. Oliver found you. Remember? This new soul will likely do the same."

"What makes you think that?"

She stands, walking over to the table she has her water bottle on to take a drink before saying, "It's easy to love and trust you. I'd like to think that I had a hand in helping you become that way. What made Oliver different is that he helped you trust yourself. He taught you just as much as you taught him. A love like that isn't easy to find."

My eyebrows pinch as I think about my late friend. "There is no one like him. I couldn't possibly find that again."

"You don't have to. You learned that lesson. There is something else you need."

"What's that?"

"I don't know. But I'm excited to see what your next friend will teach you."

There have been fewer and fewer days that Wayne has come into the office lately. With both Bentley and I here working together for the most part now, there isn't a big need for him to show up. He's here today to look over the cases that have ended up on his desk because they need a second opinion or his expertise.

That has been a blessing with how the other lead vet tech and I have been. Anyone with eyes could tell that there is something different about us. The more Bentley lets me in, the more I can see how similar we are. The more I want to help him as he struggles. My heart goes out to him because his struggles aren't deserved, though he feels differently.

I used to wonder what Wayne does with his time, but not as much any more. My brain has been filled with planning an adoption event, decorating my new place and finding time to learn more about Lee's very toned body.

I've got to push all that away because my reason for being here needs my complete attention.

My boss's office door is only partially closed when I step up to it. I twiddle my fingers for a few moments to try and steady my nerves. My heart is kicking against my ribs hard enough that I likely won't need to knock with my hand. Bentley is off today, so I have no reason to be nervous.

I'm doing this for him.

It's the right thing to do.

I'm positive of that.

Still, I'm half afraid that Bentley will not like that I'm going around him in this way.

I don't end up having to knock because Wayne looks up from his desk and sees me standing there like a creep.

Great start, Z.

My stomach twists with the realization that I am about to do what I set out to do.

Deep breath in.

I step through the door and by the look on my face, Wayne matches mine with concern. "Are you alright?"

"Yea. Yes. I'm okay." I swipe some flyaway curls from my face, more out of nervous habit than necessity. "Can I talk to you for a minute?"

He closes the file on his desk and sits back in the office chair. The creak of the leather is loud to my ears as I'm beginning to lose my nerve.

Offhandedly, I wonder why I didn't do this on my off time instead of at work. Then I remember exactly what the Thomas house is like on the weekends. There was always the possibility that any of his siblings would be there. Or worse, that Bentley would be there.

"Is there something you need for the adoption drive tomorrow?" Wayne guesses.

I wish that it were something that miniscule. How I got to that feeling about the event is beyond me. That was the most pressing problem I was facing not that long ago. And now...

"Oh, no. It's nothing to do with that." Taking the seat in the client chair across from him. "I actually need to talk to you about Bentley."

His jaw sets, "If this is about his work lately—"

"It's not," I cut him off before he can say something disparaging about his son. I know for a fact that Bentley has been doing better either way.

I move forward on my seat, sitting just at the edge to close the distance between us. "It's about something personal. And... And I'm fully aware that I'm sticking my nose where it doesn't belong..."

That gets his attention. His eyes tighten at the corners just a bit, but he asks, "What personal matter do you need to share with me about my son?"

Well, there is no turning back now.

Someone has to do it and I think there is no way that Bentley could keep going on with this wedge just driving deeper and deeper between the two of them.

Out with it, Z.

"He strongly suspects that you aren't," I take another deep breath in, trying to speak over my racing heart pounding in my chest, "That you aren't his birth father."

My boss's mouth opens for a moment and then snaps shut.

"Bentley got his original birth certificate and you weren't on it," I say. I keep my voice even, though I am bracing for the impact. I've started and I can't stop talking now that I've started spilling what I know. "He has been holding onto that information for a while and I know that it's affected him more than he's letting on."

Even that feels like a massive understatement. None of this is my place to say, but I certainly can't speak to exactly how much all of this is hurting him. I hope that in me starting this conversation, they can let each other in on the pain they both have.

"Stop," my boss snaps. "You have no right to dig into my family's business."

"I didn't dig," I say, heat rising from my heart to my face. "Bentley told me when he felt like he had no one else to talk to about this. This entire experience has been upsetting for him. You let him think that every mistake he's made while he's been trying to come to terms with a truth you kept from him was proof that he wasn't good enough. For you. Not for this clinic. He's been hurting over this and he hasn't felt comfortable coming to you to talk about it."

Wayne is silent. But the weight of what I've said and the realization that I've made is too loud in my own ears.

"He thinks that your love is conditional. He thinks that if he fails at this competition that you've put him in, that he will be replaced. As much as I hate the idea of nepotism in the workplace, there is no reason why Bentley shouldn't have this role when you leave."

"You're wrong," Wayne finally says, but there is no conviction in it. His voice is both light and distracted as he murmurs. "Lee is my son."

Unwilling to hear whatever else he has to say about this matter, I stand from my chair. "Whatever the truth is, that doesn't mean that you don't matter to him," I add. "But it does mean he deserves the truth."

My words hang between us though I know that I could expand on this more. Tell him more of my opinion, but I've done enough already. I need to get back to work. Now that I've brought this up, Wayne is bound to have this conversation with Bentley and they can resolve whatever it is that they broke.

"He does," Wayne finally concedes.

"So, you'll talk to him?" The hope is unmistakable in my voice. I can't help it. I just want to help him.

"That's none of your concern," he says in a monotone.

He's right. "It never was my business until the two of you made it so. I worked hard to make sure this adoption drive will be as good as I always remembered it being. But this is my two weeks notice."

He blinks a few times. "Y-You're quitting?" The question sounds strange in my ears because I'm never one to back down from anything.

"I have to."

Chapter 23

Lee

On my off days, I try to maximize my relaxation. It had been a while since I felt relaxed, but I feel like I've crossed a new checkpoint with Zadie. I'd stayed the night at her flat and we rolled in the sheets another time before both of us fell asleep. I woke up with her in my arms and it felt right.

Managed to even make it out of the apartment without my sister seeing me and asking a million questions I don't have the answer to. Kasey sees and notices far too much for it to be safe for me to do anything without her inquisition.

I find myself wishing that I was spending the day with Zadie like we had before. It's not a bad idea, honestly.

The thought grows stronger as I roll up to the café we ate at before and get something to bring back to her on her lunch break.

When I park in the employee lot at the back of the clinic, I see that Dad is working today. No matter, I'm not here to see him anyway. I'll be talking to him soon enough. A few more days of the awkward tension between us is nothing in comparison to the last few months.

"What's in the bag?" Korra asks me from behind the front desk when I walk in through the front entrance. "And why are you here?"

"I just brought something for—" I don't finish that thought because I know if I do, Korra will make a much bigger deal out of it and likely get my other sisters in on the gossip. "Where's Zadie?"

"Zadie?" She raises a suspicious eyebrow at me. "Why do you want to know where she is? And what is in that bag?"

She reaches out with her pen to try and take a peek inside. I pull my bag away from the counter and take a step just to be safe from her prying.

"Is she with somebody?"

Korra allows me to shift the conversation easily enough. "Not for another twenty or so. She's around here somewhere."

"Thanks," I say, going through the half door to look for her.

When I don't find her in the break room I try some of the other areas. I'm halfway down the hall when I hear my name.

Bentley got his original birth certificate and you weren't on it.

Oh, god.

He has been holding onto that information for a while and I know that it's affected him more than he's letting on.

There is nothing that could make me stick around to hear her twist the knife in my back any deeper.

I don't bother disposing of the pie. Letting it fall from my hand in the lot before I kick off the stands and drive home.

What was that?

With everything we'd done, I thought we had turned a new leaf–that maybe we were on the same page for once.

How could I be so stupid to think that she was trying to meet me where I am?

How could I be so stupid to think that I was going to tell this woman that I wanted more with her?

How could I be so stupid to fuck around and fall in love with her?

CHAPTER 24

Zadie

It seems that luck is on my side. Or maybe the weather forecast was finally right for once. When I picked this date, I knew in my heart that it was right. I'm not in my scrubs since I'm not working with any of the animals today. My cream and red sweater is lightweight over the tank top I chose to allow for the sweet breeze of spring to keep me cool. My chucks are doing double duty in serving to protect my feet from the slightly damp grass and potential puppy paws. I know for a fact that I will be visiting a certain booth that was my idea today.

Hint—it's a kissing booth, but for puppies! I'm so ready for it. Maybe I'll find a friend of my own.

As I arrive at the park that we've booked for the day, I park Lemon and immediately head to the covered basketball court to get a good look at the place. It won't look this empty for long. I'm here about thirty minutes before all the equipment, tables, tents and volunteers should be arriving. Thomas clinic staff doesn't have to be here until shortly before the drive begins, so I'm on my own for the time being.

Bentley should be here soon enough, but I don't want to wait for him to start. The extra-large plastic storage container with the supplies I purchased isn't too heavy to carry over here. I heft it out of my trunk and take out my carefully marked cones to designate where everyone should be setting up.

I get through about seven of them before I hear his truck pulling up to the parking lot. The silly little smile on my face is not welcome right now because I know there is a full day of stress ahead of me, but I am a little happy that I'll get to see him before all of that really sets in.

Placing the eight cones in place for the puppy smooching booth, I have a little skip in my step as I reach the big blue truck. "Morning," I say, giving him a little salute.

"Yea," is all he says, walking past me to the tent.

Stunned, I'm stuck right where I was watching him walk over to the court in a long sleeved tee and jeans.

Who pissed in his Cheerios?

I shake my head, letting his attitude go. In just under five everyone should be getting here. Easier said than done, but I don't have a choice. I'll just ask him about it when the event is over.

First to arrive are the tables, and thank goodness for that because food, supplies and documentation come immediately after.

Korra is on the task of getting the adoption paperwork for the new friends leaving with their owners today. She comes over with a bright smile and her signature rose pen in hand. "Hey, girl! I'm ready for this! Are you?"

I put a hand in my back pocket and set my hip to the side. "As ready as I'll ever be! I'm only directing right now."

"Yea, you are," she says. "And looking good doing it," she adds with a wink.

I'm glad she thinks so. I certainly don't feel like it. Everything is going just as Bentley and I planned it.

This is good.

This is great, even.

The event will start soon and people are going to arrive. Most importantly, these animals are going to find their forever homes today. That is what matters.

It doesn't matter how many times I repeat that in my head, I still feel that Bentley is missing.

Where is he?

Taking stock in my mental checklist of who should be where around the park, it looks amazing. All the booths and tables are set up. The Adoption Event Banner is hung high over it all.

Still I can't find where this man is.

Soft music plays through the space as people begin to explore what the event has to offer. The faint smell of pizza wafts on the breeze from one of the food trucks we hired. I smile and greet guests and adoptees a plenty. A few of our patients are here with their owners looking for playmates.

On my rounds, I make it back to my storage container. It's there in the supply tent that I find Bentley helping a volunteer set up a cat adoption kit.

"There you are," I say, a sense of relief coming over me with finding him. "Have you been here the whole time?"

"I've been all over helping the volunteers," he says, undeterred from his task of putting supplies in the temporary cat carrier.

He's technically a coordinator like me. I don't understand why he's been with the volunteers. "Why?"

He must be done with his prep because he just looks at me for a moment before grabbing another carrier. "Did you need something?" His tone is so cold and now I can't ignore it.

"Is something wrong?"

That makes him pause. His head tilts heavily to one side as he studies me like I've said something very stupid. "Should something be wrong?"

"Can we talk in private real quick?" I ask, not wanting whatever this is to be exchanged over the heads of all these people.

"You're really good at that, huh?" His murmur is not missed by me.

Looping his arm with my own, I usher us to the opposite side of the court where no one is hanging around. "What is your problem?" I gesture with my arm towards the area we just came from. "What was that?"

He shakes his head, taking his arm from mine. "Still you act like you're Little Miss Perfect. Do you ever turn the facade off?"

"What?" I snap. "What does that mean?"

He sneers, "You think I didn't hear your little talk with my Dad?"

The blood drains from my face. "You-you heard that?"

"Oh, yeah," he says. "I heard how you tried to shit-talk me to him and get ahead. I understand that finding a job can be hard these days, but the lengths you're willing to go through is... I don't know. I'm a fool sometimes, but no one makes me feel more like a fool than you do. *Congratulations.*"

"What?" This time it comes out as a whisper. "I don't know what you're talking about. If you heard me talking to your Dad then—"

"*Bentley got his original birth certificate and you weren't on it,*" he says in a tone that is supposed to be mine. "*He has been holding onto that information for a while and I know that it's affected him more than he's letting on.*" He leans close to my face, "You not only took away my choice to talk to my Dad about this on my own terms, but you used it to plead your case in taking over for him." His tone rises though not loud enough to alarm someone, it's enough to prick my skin with goosebumps. "Since I'm not his *real kid*, we're on equal standing, right? You can come in and get what you always wanted. No obstruction from me." He takes a step away from me. "Fine. I'm not playing this game anymore. It's yours. I'll fall back since that's what you want."

"I—I don't," I splutter, my thoughts too chaotic to articulate anything of value. "Bentley, you don't understand. I was just—"

"Save it. Really. I just want to finish up here so I can go home," he bites out, brushing past me.

For several moments I just stand there. I don't know what to do. There is too much that I should say that I didn't. That I couldn't.

I've messed everything up.

Chapter 25

Lee

"Are you ready for this?"

No. There is no way I can be.

With Zadie taking all the air from under my wings, I don't feel ready for this at all. It wasn't like I was going for shock factor or getting some sort of "gotcha" moment on camera. But I know it doesn't feel right going to have this conversation after he already knows what I suspect of him.

After what Zadie said, I expected him to reach out to me at this point, but he didn't.

There is so much I have to say and questions that I want to ask him. For months they have only been piling up. This is finally the time for me to be able to do that.

"As ready as I'll ever be," I tell Korra before we walk in together.

My other siblings are already inside, bar Nia who is still on campus. I could use a hug from her, but at this point I don't want to distract her when she's so close to graduating.

Entering the living room is more charged than I could have prepared for. Zach and Korra flank my Dad on the couch. Korra joins Kasey's side sitting on the arm near her. The only place for me to choose is the chair across from them to have this conversation. I don't think too much about the placement of everyone since that isn't what's important.

After taking my seat, I just say what I came to say. There is no need for any build up. The room is already tense enough.

"I'm sure you already know why everyone is here. I'll just say what has been on my mind." From my back pocket, I pull out the envelope that holds the damning document that at one point glared at me from my own coffee table for weeks on end. "Your name isn't on my original birth certificate. Why is that?" My words sound cold, even to my own ears, but I don't have a polite way to suggest what's on my mind.

My Dad takes a look at the envelope but doesn't reach to open it. He simply looks me in the eyes, saying, "It's not there." He sighs long and hard. "It's not there because by blood, I'm not your father."

Though we all suspected that it was true, it doesn't keep everyone from gasping at his response. I nod my head, the truth of his words not giving me the peace that I hoped they would. "How long have you known?"

"Long before you were born. Your mother and I," His eyes go glossy just saying her name. "Our relationship was never meant to happen. She was engaged to a man long before I met her. He wasn't around though. He was deployed and he had no plan on coming back. They broke the engagement on amicable terms and I thought nothing of it. The woman I loved was free to love me back. We had you," He says looking at Zach. "And then we welcomed the twins into our lives." He squeezes their hands. "It was all we planned for. Three kids. But shortly before the twins were born, Aiden came back." He shakes his head.

"You knew him? You knew my birth-father?"

"I did," he says, jaw working. "He-he called himself her friend. At the time, your mother was working at the reception desk of one of the, now closed, facilities for the Brenford's. This plant specialized in processing steel parts. Somehow, Aiden also got a job there."

I don't know how to feel about the direction of this recollection, but I remain quiet so that he can get all of it out. It seems that everyone else is enraptured with the story as well.

"Your Mom couldn't see what I could. That man was still in love with her. But she defended him. They grew up together. That was her best friend. I was seeing everything all wrong."

"Were you?" Kasey asks. I know she had read through many of Mom's journals. The writer in her constantly wanting to find romance in anything.

His head hangs. "No. I knew I wasn't."

The bang of the door startles all of us as Bryce comes into the living room. His eyes dart around looking for his fiancé and then me.

"You won't believe this, but all that we know about the Kindrick case just got messier," Bryce says, and then winces when he realizes what is happening right now. "I can, oh, I'll just wait."

"No, you won't," I say. "What do you mean it got messier?"

He pulls his laptop out. "One of the documents that was finally able to be viewed because the NDA is expired. I mean, that was a long agreement, but I don't think they expected to be in the position they are currently in. This is going to set so much up for us in a positive way." He looks around the table, "Goes without saying that none of this can leave this room. However, I think you'd want to know this before the public does."

"Want us to know what?" My Dad asks, brows creasing.

Bryce looks around at all of us. "Delanna was forced to conceal the true father of her unborn baby."

"Why the hell would she do that?" Kasey asks, fully invested in this turn of events.

"He died in one of the long closed facilities. She was the one to discover his body and alert someone to help them. Aiden had passed before emergency vehicles had arrived and the Brenfords have been working hard to keep it under wraps now that those NDAs are expiring one by one. The legal action the Brenfords are facing that has derailed all their usual business is being funded by the Kindrick family in the name of justice," he shrugs as if it's to be expected, "and as a bid to move the Brenfords from their seat of power in this town."

"Go back to the concealing. Why would they force Mom to do that?" I stand, asking the question that is the most important. "What kind of leverage could they have on her?"

My Dad is the one to speak up instead of Bryce. "Me. I was their leverage." We all turn to face him. It's only shocking news coming from the man who I thought I knew everything about.

"How could you be the leverage?" Korra asks, now sitting in the lap of Bryce who has taken the other chair in the living room. "You know what happened to Aiden?"

"I do. You see, that building was old and I don't think anything was up to code. Lanna complained about it and wrote them reports on the conditions, constantly. It was her job to file for repairs or whatever. The day he passed, I remember clearly. There was a collapse on one of the floors that sent steel crashing through a wall and crushed several employees, including Aiden. Some who were only badly injured. I didn't know she was pregnant. She likely didn't either until they took her to the hospital."

A tear falls from my Dad's eye. He wipes it away, looking down at his wedding band that he still wears. Twisting the ring, his voice is thick when he says, "She knew that the baby wasn't mine. We argued that night. It was awful, but she went to the Brenfords the next day with everything she knew and made the mistake of revealing that she was carrying Bentley and who his father was. They dismissed her threats and issued one of their own." He looks into my eyes, "You see, I was a young hopeful man, just starting a practice to pay off this home and it was them who could take all of that away if they so chose. They'd blackball us and ostracize our family. There was nothing we could do to stop them so she had to make a choice to protect the interest of her family instead of avenging the man she once loved."

"Shit," Kasey says, but we're all thinking it.

"So that must be why she kept that tie and the ID. Oh gross. So it was definitely blood then. Oh god, Lee..." Korra trails off.

"No, I knew he was gone. It's not the kind of story that you want to hear, but it is still my truth. Part of it anyway. At least I have something of his."

"You should really read the journals, Lee. Mom spoke fondly of Aiden," Kasey adds, giving Dad a sheepish look since we already know what happened there.

My Dad pats my hand. "Zadie was right. You deserved to know the truth, but I was afraid even after all this time that I could lose everything. I had no idea that you were having doubts or trying to put things together on your own. I had no idea why you were behaving the way you were. It was always your mother who could see these things better than me. I really don't know what I'm doing without her guidance. I know I need to be better."

"Zadie said that?"

"Right before she put in her two weeks. She told me that you should have always been my first choice and she's right. You should have been."

She said that? Wait, "She put in her two weeks? She's leaving?"

Chapter 26

Lee

The Harmony Hill Defense Group is rather unassuming in comparison to what I imagine the massive skyscraper he used to work out of looked like. There are only a few cars parked here. Two of which I recognize as Bryce and Wynn's cars. The others I don't. Even in this small town there is something to surprise me.

I've taken the weekend to figure out what I'm going to do about everything I learned. The desire for information about my parents has been riding me hard since December and now that I know, I can't go back to that time when I didn't know anything.

Do I want that ignorance again? I *don't*.

As blissful as it was, the truth of my parentage holds a weight that I couldn't understand before. There is so much to process and one person who I know could unlock many more truths for me.

Kasey came to my condo to bring the journals that she knew had my Mom's recollection about the man that I know for sure is my birth-father now.

At some point I'll be strong enough to read through those.

Remembering his voice from that recording and trying to connect his tragic end is more than enough to wrap my head around at present. I wish that I could recover faster, but I can't. It's never been my forte unfortunately.

More than anything else, I wish I had not waited so long to say something to my Dad.

That wedge between us wasn't entirely of my own making, but I knew it was there. I should have gone with my gut and asked him when Korra showed me that ID. Months that I lost without being able to have peace.

If not peace, then just making my way towards understanding.

Months that I thought poorly of my Mom. Every memory I had was being turned in my mind, searching for something that I wouldn't find. I don't know that I agree with everything she did, but she did her best.

She loved me–Dad too. They both loved me and I felt like the truth they kept from me was an affront, an attack, on me. Who knows if there was a better choice when I wasn't there to know the kind of pressure they were experiencing in this situation.

The Brenfords are not the kind of people to let anything shed a negative light on them. It has only been in recent years that their perception in this town has even begun to turn.

Taking the keys from my ignition, I take a deep inhale and resolve myself to the fact that I'm taking this next step.

The receptionist, Marie, pages Bryce when I get inside. This is the first time that I have been in this building, so I'm not sure exactly where he conducts business. It's on me to wait for him to come back and get me. I try not to fidget as I wait for him.

"You ready?" Bryce asks me when he finally comes from the long hallway. It's become a phrase that I just have to be very cautious of at this point. *I don't have a choice.* Everything will happen regardless of my level of preparation.

I need to do this.

"Yeah, let's do it," I say, following him down a hall to the only open door.

Bryce stands in the doorway, blocking his client inside. "Remember what I told you."

I nod in understanding because he is doing me a huge favor by setting this up.

When I walk into the room, I'm stunned to see the man sitting in the chair on the far right of the room. By the time I'm inside, he stands.

The resemblance between him and my late birth-father isn't as strong as I was expecting, but it's clear that they are related in some way.

"Shep," he says, holding a hand out to me. "Good to meet you, man," he says.

I shake his hand. "Lee," I introduce myself in return. "Thank you for meeting with me."

"No problem. I really was interested to meet you when Bryce told me who you were. There's a lot we have to talk about."

Running a hand over my beard, I say, "A lot is right. I have so many questions."

"Well, I can answer quite a few of them right away. I didn't really know Uncle Aiden since I was barely a year old when he passed. Our family remembers his passing though. It's one of the many things that we won't let slide."

I didn't think about the fact that my birth-father's passing would affect more than just me. In some way it makes me happy to know that he was loved and cared for by someone besides my Mom.

"It seems that the Kindricks have a lot on their hands in that front."

Shep adjusts his collar before continuing. "You're right. We do. My grandfather is still alive and well. He remembers what this town once was and though we've been gone, that time has passed. I'm just the first of many of us on our arrival back in town."

There will be more Kindricks in town? "You have this restaurant. What's the story with that?"

"It's always been our way. We had a restaurant before that was just for comfort cooking. That's not really my style. I prefer something more modern. Contrary to popular belief, towns this size, enjoy new options and tend to appreciate that close to home."

I don't doubt what he's saying, but I'm still confused on why he's so adamant when the Brenfords have made it hell for him to start his restaurant here.

"I see that look. I get it. I could open the restaurant anywhere, so why cause a fuss here? The answer is simple. We're taking Harmony Hill back. Kindricks are no longer stepping aside. Especially with new developments like what truly happened to my uncle are the tip of the iceberg." He looks to Bryce for some sort of signal and Bryce nods his head. "With your help, I'd like to continue exposing this family for what they truly are and boot them from this town for good."

"How could I possibly help with that? Besides, they are one of the largest employers around. There is no way that you could kick them out for good."

He winks at me. *Winks*. "Just let me and Bryce worry about that. The only thing I need from you is a true testimony about how the loss of your father has affected you. I realize you didn't know him, but I'm sure him being gone has had an impact, right?"

His words aren't untrue though they hurt all the same. "I don't know if I'm ready for people to find out that I'm not Wayne's birth-son just yet."

Shep seems to understand as he nods and stands from his seat. "I see. I don't need an answer right away. All I ask is that you'll think about it. Everything that happened to Aiden is enough to get a jury to sympathize. But hearing from you... that would be another nail in the coffin."

I feel dismissed as he continues to stand. I didn't get the answers I wanted, but I did learn more than I had before.

Isn't that always the way though?

Bryce stands with Shep to say. "Wayne already told you his account of what he knew about the incident that cost Aiden his life, but I have permission from Shep here to share anything related to the case that I can. It appears that there is more to that night than we bargained for. I'm confident that as evidence continues to mount against them, we'll get what we're looking for."

I'm the only one sitting at this point. Pushing off from the table, I get to my feet. "I'll help you both in any way that I can if it means that my father will get the justice he deserves and if it will benefit the town, that's even better."

Shep shakes my hand again. "Love to hear it. Let's take Brenford down."

Once I'm back in my truck, I let everything that has happened settle. There's a strange hollowness from mourning a man I never knew. A hole where a sense of duty and hope that I never had before now resides.

I can't call it grief in the same way that I grieve my Mom, but I can acknowledge that what happened to Aiden was deeply sad. That his family was probably also wronged by the same people who are notoriously wronging the citizens of this town.

It was something that before, I couldn't understand but I'm starting to see that I wasn't immune from the malice of their touch.

Because of them, I never knew my birth-father. Aiden will only ever be an idea in my mind. Though that loss is contained to me in the Thomas family, every single one of our lives have been touched by the Brenfords. We're a part of this community and I'm determined to be on the right side of our history.

My Dad's face comes to mind then.

I think of Wayne and how he tried to teach me what he knew. Of how he gave me the opportunity to earn what he has worked so hard to build. How he took me under his wing even though he knew that I was not biologically his. How he loved me anyway and tried his best.

It wasn't perfect but none of us are.

And like always it seems, Zadie's words come back to mind.

Your memories will always be yours. You can look back on them fondly and savor the happiness.

I want to savor these moments with my Dad while he's here. I want to remember the good times that we had together.

I want to do what's best for his legacy, even if it means that I'm getting less. But especially if it means that Zadie is getting more.

I pick up my phone and call my Dad. When the line connects, I ask, "Hey. Do you have a minute to talk? I want to talk about the future."

Chapter 27

Zadie

It's weird knowing that there is just over a week of time left where I'll be working here. Even still I go through all the motions as usual.

What other choice do I have?

It's clear that Bentley wants nothing to do with me anymore. I haven't gotten a call or a text from him since the adoption event. I don't expect to at this point.

Obviously, he overheard what I said to his Dad and still he hates me. I couldn't just leave with this big gaping issue between the two of them.

Sure, it wasn't my place to say anything, but he absolutely could have said something over these past three months, but instead he let it fester and turn into this wound that he didn't know how to heal.

Korra turns the engagement ring on her finger, when she asks me. "You're still going to be around for the wedding right?"

Leaning against the half door, I assure her, "Of course, babe. Nothing has changed on that front. I'm going to be here for you. Just not at work."

The look my friend gives me is more than telling of her emotions. "You know I wish you had told me that you were leaving first."

I chuckle at the twist of her lips as she pouts. "Why's that?"

"Because I would have talked you out of it. Isn't that obvious?"

A rich laugh bubbles out of my chest at her ridiculous self. "It's not that simple. You know it's been just a mess with the two of us here. I think your brother was going to explode if this decision didn't happen the way it did."

"Forget about Lee. What about me?"

I smile at her though it feels flat on my face. "Like I said, I'll still be here for you in every other way."

"I'm glad you said that." She reaches under her desk to produce a bag that she holds in her hands. "I have something pretty niche to ask of you while we have this break in between patients."

Eyeing the bag, I say, "I'll bite. What's in the bag?"

"I've just been feeling really weird lately. And though my period is irregular—it's never been late." She drops the bag on the counter and I can clearly see what's inside of it.

"So that's why you're holding an entire drugstore bag of pregnancy tests?" She smuggled it in here like contraband. I suppose in your family's workplace it likely is.

Especially when all of the family members who do work here are men.

She nods emphatically. "I'd feel a lot better if we took it together. I know for a fact you're not so it's kind of like a control."

"Sweetheart, I love where your head's at, but I don't think that's how that works. I am happy to take one at the same time you're taking it... if that makes you feel less nervous."

"I mean, it really would." Korra puts the rose pen in her hair when she stands from her desk. "It's not that I don't wanna have kids with Bryce. Because I think our babies would be absolutely beautiful. Can you imagine those genes? I could daydream about babies for sure. But I also know that we're getting married in a few months. We're in the final processes of planning that. I need to know if I'm planning for a dress that's gonna accommodate a belly bump, you know?"

"Yep. I'm hearing you."

"Okay, let's go then!" She squeezes my hand as she pulls me toward the staff bathroom in the back.

The bell rings just as we're returning to the front. Chad Michael Purray is here for his check up just in time.

"I've got it from here," I say to Nitra, while Korra continues to stare in stunned excitement. Her eyes have not reduced in size since she look at the positive stick in the bathroom. She has quite a bit to think about right now.

I do too.

It's all I can do is think about what I've done and if I can live with the consequences of that.

It wasn't my place to tell Wayne and I knew that going in to speak for him. What hurts the most is that he thinks I did what I did to get ahead when my intention was never to hurt him.

If only I could just get a chance to talk to him and apologize for stepping over the line and clarify that I only had good intentions in telling his big secret...

When I get Chad Michael back to the examination table, it's obvious that this cat is very, very pissed to be here and now it's my problem to deal with. Nitra sits in the far corner doing something on her phone as I do what I'm supposed to.

His ears flatten the second I slide my hands under his belly and he lets out an annoyed meow that sounds like he's trying to speak to me. Or better yet, tell me off. He's orange, overweight and dramatic. "Hey," I murmur, settling him back onto the table. "I know. I'm not having the best day either." Chad growls in response when I check his gums despite his bad attitude.

It's been a slow day and that has meant that I have way too much time with my thoughts. With just a week left, I've got to accept that the future I thought was incoming will look different than the one I hoped for. I have options. Of course, I do. But I didn't want options. I wanted this to be my place. To belong here.

Adjusting my stethoscope, I listen to his heartbeat and time it with my watch. Funny how animals never have to apologize for taking up space. They don't wonder if they've ruined something by caring too much or acting too soon. They certainly don't replay conversations at three in the morning trying to dissect every word for intent or meaning.

It must be nice. Lucky little things.

"You don't get attached," I tell the cat quietly. "That's the trick."

He blinks at me, thoroughly unimpressed by the advice I've given him.

I scratch behind Chad's ears, completing his exam so that he can be on his way back home where he'd rather be. At least I can still be a friend to these furry guys for a little while longer.

I could have sworn that I did the right thing by giving my notice and getting out of their hair. Bentley doesn't agree since he hasn't even commented on it.

One thing is for certain though. I'm not running. I've already started looking at other small clinics that need help within an hour radius of my flat. He might not have to see me, but I am not going to leave my new place. That's just tough for him. I mounted things to my wall. Its mounted. That is as permanent as it gets.

I'll find something. I always do.

Finishing my notes on Chad's condition, I share what I can with Nitra and slide the cat back into his carrier. He immediately swats at me through the grate, but it's lazy and half-hearted at best.

"Yea. I probably deserve that," I tell him before Nitra laughs with me and I walk them back up front with Korra.

The metal of the exam table is cold under my hands as I lean on it for support. The ache that swells in my chest is pressing too insistently to ignore. I just need to breathe through it for a moment longer before I can face anyone else right now.

The only reason my heart aches this way is because I loved him. Loved him in pieces and glances and parts. He had his own way of showing his care and I knew that he worked hard to protect what was soft and sensitive about himself. Neither of our intentions really meant anything when it came down to it.

Intentions aren't enough.

Being at this clinic everyday will just hurt too much. It's not about him getting the role over me at all anymore. It's about losing that understanding that we were learning how to be with each other and all of that is gone. The thing we were building is nothing. I don't know how to make my mind or body accept that. No amount of yoga can fix that.

Finally, I straighten and smooth my scrub top before checking the schedule for who's next. One more appointment before lunch and then I can go get a loaded sundae.

My phone buzzes in my pocket and I ignore it at first. I don't want to talk to anyone but the animals right now.

Then it buzzes again and I pull it out of my pocket.

Lee: You're leaving the clinic?

Lee: We need to talk.

Chapter 28

Lee

A Tuesday like any other except this one feels wrong.

For one, I've come to terms with the fact that I am an honorary Thomas son. There is nothing derogatory about that. This is family but my history is different. I think that will bring change that I couldn't foresee being positive. My hope is that it will be.

For two, I'm no longer in competition with Zadie McLane for the role of Veterinarian at Thomas & Friends.

For three, there is a notable difference in her behavior toward me now that I'm here. Where there was back-and-forth turned sneaky kisses in the break room, there's nothing. It's dead space. She's careful to avoid me and goes out of her way to give me space when we are working together. She didn't respond to my text, but I know she got it.

The biggest change is the fourth thing. Now, I've made a point of saying how little I enjoy snooping. And I still do! But in the coat room, something fell out of Zadie's huge purse. I did not, and I repeat—did not, go looking for this. I was simply putting my coat on the hanger when it clattered to the floor.

A pregnancy test.

A positive pregnancy test.

I've never shoved anything back as quickly as I did that thing.

So many thoughts are running through my mind at once. I'm not sure if this could be something that happened to me. I'm well aware that a vasectomy isn't a one-hundred percent fail safe. But I think it was at least gonna be safer than this.

How in the fuck did I get Zadie pregnant?

And why the fuck has she not told me?

And she's still leaving the clinic but hasn't said anything!

I know that what we have is rocky and we haven't been on the best terms as of late. I recognize that it's a gross understatement. There are many things to talk to her about. I feel all different kinds of ways about this whole situation but she's pregnant?

I need to make this right.

Everything really started with her cider and those cookies.

If it weren't for that, I don't know how my life would have changed. I need to call in the big guns to help me rectify this. Pulling out my phone, I tap the contact before I have a chance to second guess myself.

"Kasey, I need you to help me with this."

My sister's droll voice is as sarcastic as ever, "Tell me about it. I have notes–"

"I don't have time for the snark. Are you going to help me or not? I might have fucked all this up."

Her sigh is loud over the receiver. "Yeah, you did. Honestly, Lee, what were you thinking?"

"I was... Look, I don't have time to get into all that. I need to fix things with Zadie."

By the time my sisters leave, the condo smells like clean linen and subtly of the flowers that have been placed around.

There is nothing wrong in asking for help when you need it. I had to own that and be at the mercy of Korra and Kasey's planning. I'm normally not one for a staged kind of vibe, but I wanted everything to be as close to perfect as I could manage to win my girl back.

Lighting the candles until the room has a more warm glow instead of the stark overhead lighting, it looks like I know what I'm doing when I don't. I'm just hoping that it's not too late.

The knock comes sooner than I expected but I'm ready.

When I open the door, there she is. Zadie's not in her scrubs from work but her hair is still pulled back into a low bun with a soft sweater and tights. I want to drag her into a hug, but I know that would be entirely inappropriate.

Her eyes flick to the scene behind me and then they soften when she looks back toward me. "Bentley," she says. It's just my name, but there is a fragility that I'm not used to in her tone.

I step to the side. "Please come in." There is so much to discuss and we don't need to do it in this doorway.

The door closes behind her with a quiet click and suddenly the condo feels too small for everything that presses between us.

"I should have answered your texts," she says, shifting from foot to foot.

Taking a seat on the couch, I beckon her over to sit as well. "I understand why you didn't." Which was true, even if I didn't like it.

The candles flicker on the table, illuminating the blush roses there. Looking down at her hands, she says, "I owe you an apology. A real one."

My chest tightens but I don't interrupt her when I shift closer to her on the cushion. The heat from her thigh is close enough to feel though I wish we were closer.

"I thought I was helping you, protecting you. I figured that if I got ahead of the situation then you wouldn't get hurt. Or get more hurt by everything. I didn't listen to the reasoning in my head that told me it wasn't my place."

"No," I say quietly, waiting for her to meet my eyes again. "You didn't."

The tears are shining in her eyes when she continues, "I'm sorry for taking your choice away. I'm sorry for breaking your trust in me... for assuming that I knew what you needed instead of talking to you about it."

Reaching for her hand, she pulls it away. The rejection of that one move hits me and I put my hand back on my own leg. "I can't go back on my decision to leave the clinic. I didn't mean to keep it from you. I never meant to leave without saying anything to you about it. I just–once I realized how badly I'd messed up, staying felt like salt in a wound. I couldn't handle that every day."

It's taking everything in me not to reach for her again. Especially after her words hit me in that broken tone she has. I resist the urge and say my piece. "What you did behind my back—hurt. But not as much as you leaving without telling me. Not as much as you thinking I didn't deserve to hear that from you."

"You did deserve to hear it from me. I know that..." Her voice trails off. "I just didn't trust myself to actually leave when I wanted this place for myself so badly. With you and with the clinic."

Silence settles in the space but it's thoughtful as we both appreciate what's been shared already.

I'm surprised my voice is steady when I say, "I have my own things to say. Things that I need you to hear from me." This time when I reach for her hand, she lets me. "I talked to Dad about what actually happened that day when I overheard you talking to him. Of course I was angry with what I heard, but I now know I didn't hear everything. You didn't have to leave. You shouldn't have felt like you had to when all of this was my shit to deal with and I wasn't doing a great job of it. I guess I still felt like that kid that was always racing behind you, just trying to keep up. I was already aware of how hard I was falling for you despite everything I was going through. I didn't know how to ask for what I wanted when I thought that competing was more important to you."

Big green orbs look back at me from the moment I said I was falling for her, but I have to keep going. "I don't want to compete. I want to have something that doesn't disappear the second one of us stumbles. I want someone who sees me for who I am and stays regardless." Standing from the couch, I hold my hand out for her again. There is something else that I'd like her to see.

We walk over to the bar where I have the folder open. She doesn't look at the paperwork at first. She's too busy marveling at the short vase beside it. "Where did you find poinsettias at this time of year?"

"I had a little help from the twins, but since there were so many in the house that day, I needed them to say what I was going to say." The candle light flickers over our faces as she falls against me. The fit is perfect. Her forehead rests against my chest and my hand rubs circles on her back.

"You have said a lot," she jokes. "I know you're long-winded, but jeez, you can really talk."

Holding her chin between my fingers, I hold her face so that she's looking at me again. "But I haven't said the most important thing."

"What's that?"

"I love you. As much as I didn't want that to be true all along, I do. I'm hoping that I haven't ruined everything for us and the baby."

She pushes off of me in a quick movement. "Baby?" She questions. "What baby?"

I scratch my jaw. "I saw the test when it fell out of your purse. It was positive as all hell. I mean, the window said positive in all caps."

Then she laughs–guffaws more like it–in her deeper register, making me more self-conscious. "No, no, no. Bentley, you've got it all wrong."

"Got what wrong?" There's nothing wrong with my eyes or my memory. I know what I saw and that test was as positive as it could be. It wasn't in my plans, but I'm going to do whatever I need to in supporting Zadie.

If we are expecting, then it's better that I acknowledge that early and prepare accordingly. I'm doing whatever is necessary to be a lasting fixture in Zadie's life moving forward.

"That wasn't my test, it was for-" she looks around after pausing. "Someone else. I have it because I'm going to make something special for the announcement."

The air rushes from between my lips. "Thank goodness. I don't know if I'm ready for kids or any of that."

Through barely restrained giggles, she says, "Bent, you got snipped. I don't think this is what miracles are made of."

"Hey," I snap, "You never know. Stranger things have happened."

She continues laughing and I grab her around the waist which only makes her laugh harder. Eventually I set her down and she leans on the bar again. Then her laughter abruptly stops.

Her brow furrows when she asks, "What is this?" Picking the folder up, she reads it more intently. "Bentley!"

"Dad is serious about retiring after Korra's wedding. He asked me if I'd take over. I told him I would-on one condition."

With wide eyes, she says, "Lee-"

"I told him that it's both of us or neither of us. Two vets. Equal say and equal ownership."

She just blinks at the paperwork, too stunned to speak. I can't help the smile stretching my cheeks.

"You'd do that?" she finally asks after a while of reading what's in the file.

"I already did," I tell her, pointing to the page. "That's my signature. It's just waiting for yours."

Throwing her arms around my neck, she kisses me fiercely, letting all the weight of everything fall behind us. "I don't know what to say," she admits, tears falling though she hasn't let go of me.

"I hope you'll say yes," I confess. "Though I understand if it's not what you want anymore."

She smacks my chest playfully. Too many emotions on her face to discern anyone in particular. After taking a deep breath she teases, "Hush. I'm going to have to get used to working together with you again."

"Yea," I say, wiping the tears from her cheek. "But tonight, we don't have to talk anymore about this."

She looks around at the romantic scene I've set in the room. The flowers, the candles and there is a dinner in the kitchen for whenever we get to it. "So, this was a setup..." she teases.

"Maybe we can get Christmas and Valentine's Day right this time," I huff, carrying her to the couch again.

CHAPTER 29

Epilogue: Lee

I'm carrying her to the couch because I don't think I could make it to the bed.

I need to feel her skin.

I need to kiss her lips.

I want to be close to her and I don't want to put any more time or distance between us.

We fall onto the couch, her knees bracketing my thighs as she leans down to nip at my neck. It's sweet and I am unhurried, but that's not the kind of vibe I'm here for right now. With both of my hands on her ass, I settle her onto my lap more fully.

Both of my hands, hold her face to mine, deepening our kiss. Slowing down how we move together. Her hands explore my body. Warm fingertips reaching under my shirt to run over my chest and down my stomach to my sides where she holds me.

That just won't do.

I break our kiss only so that I can take this shirt off. Her eyes roam over my body, retracing her early movements but now while she can see me. "I love the way you touch me," I admit.

"I love touching you. You don't know how much I thought about doing just that when I couldn't." She's careful to take her own sweater off so that it doesn't get caught on her hair. Underneath she only has a cream soft bra that her nipples are already poking through. My thumb runs over the peak of one, making it even harder under the stretchy fabric. Pressing my lips to it, I suck gently at it before taking in between my teeth. She bucks on my lap at the brief sting, moaning my name before I give the other hard point the same treatment.

When I release her, she stands from the couch to remove all the clothes that stand between us. I thought I was hard before but seeing all of Zadie's luscious curves on display is never going to be something that won't put me over the edge. I want to sink my teeth into the impression of the seam from her tights that runs down the side of her thick thigh. Good news, I've got all the time in the world to taste each dimple, curve and freckle. I'm starting here.

Pulling her back to me on the couch, I trail my tongue over that indent, using my grip on her cheeks to keep her in place even though she squirms. Her little noises as I tease her are fuel to the fire building in my lower stomach, begging me to free my dick and slide into her.

In time, I will. But for now, I want to reacquaint myself with the bounty that is Zadie McLane's body.

Her hands run through my hair while I nip and suck on every inch of skin I can reach before they settle on my beard. Using her leverage, she forces me to stop my teasing and look at her. "Take these pants off now, or so help me God—"

She's not able to finish her demand as she's flipped on her back and spread open before me. My arm holding onto her full tits and effectively giving me an unobstructed view of the part of her that I'm always eager to taste.

"Ohhh," she sighs. With one hand now holding her soft belly and the other her thigh, to keep her in place, I suck her sensitive lips into my mouth. "That's good too."

Zadie's fingers are back in my hair, guiding me to go slower or faster. I let her lead me to whatever feels best for her and she rewards me with sweet moans and sighs of pleasure.

When she's had enough, she pulls me up to her lips. No longer complacent with my pants, she's quick to get them off of me.

I allow her to crawl over me so that I'm lying back on my couch. I'm straining in my boxer briefs at this point, but it's worth it when she places sloppy kisses up my length from balls to tip. "Fuck. Zadie. You know what your mouth does to me."

She pays me back for all my teasing before finally tugging the waistband down. My dick flops out, hard and straining against my stomach. She grabs me firmly with one hand and strokes me twice before taking me into her mouth. Zadie doesn't struggle to take as much as she can but when she holds my balls in her palm squeezing slightly, I think I'm going to lose my nut.

"Goddamn, red. Fuck, I need to be inside you."

"I'm aching for you, Bent," she giggles, running the back of her hand over her mouth.

I rush her, my arms wrapped around her body, our chest beating quickly against each other before she's scrambling to straddle me again.

Our eyes hold each other as she guides me into her tight pussy. "That's it, red. Fuck, that's it."

She rocks on me slowly. It takes a little time for her body to adjust to my size, but she's loving every second as I do my best not to thrust upward into her. Oh, I want to with how she grips me like a fist.

Holding her waist, keeping our pace, her hands hold purchase on my chest at first before leaning back onto my thighs. "Oh, god, yes," she pants into my mouth when she leans in for more sloppy kisses.

What she's doing feels so good, but I want to take her harder, deeper. She's close and I can tell that she needs that little bit more to get over the edge.

I'm happy to help.

Flipping us again, I hold her thigh to my chest and give her a moment to get comfortable in the new position. Licking my thumb before rubbing it over her clit, I slide my length back inside of her to the hilt. With wide eyes, she nods, approving of the new position. I'm slow at first, only a stroke or two before I pick up the pace and grab her ass to lift her right into the position she needs to fall over the edge.

"Ohhh, like that Bentley," she whines. "Like that, like that. You've got me so close. Please..."

We're both sweating and even in the candle light I can see how her golden skin glitters with it. Everything about this woman turns me on—her voice, her heart, her body, her mind—everything, including her sweat.

"Take it, red. It's yours," I tell her between pants as she clenches harder and tighter around me.

When she climaxes, body going tight and breaths getting shallow, I make a mental image of her just like this. Breaking apart on my dick, body wracked with shudders of pleasure. It's too much to take and I follow her right over the edge, jerky movements as I chase that high of being warm and wet inside her.

Nothing compares to this and I could never find someone who could ever compete with this woman in front of me.

This woman I love.

"Don't," I say, though she reaches for her phone anyway. We've been lying on the couch talking and listening to music for a while now. At some point, I do need to feed us. I'm just not ready to move on from this moment in time yet.

She picks up, mouthing to me, "Peer review," before grinning from ear to ear. Her face still flushed from what we've done and her hair mussed up as well. She looks thoroughly fucked and it's not a bad sight, I'll admit. I can't be mad when she looks so good loved by me.

From the speaker, Kasey questions, "Why am I seeing your bright ass yellow SUV parked in front of Lee's condo?"

"Oop," Zadie says, before she bursts into a fit of giggles.

"I knew it. I called it. I'm never wrong when it comes to matters of hunching. He repeated over and over again how it wasn't like that. He was *just apologizing*. Blah blah blah. It's romantic as hell in there, if I do say so myself. Glad it worked though you all but said that you hated each other." She makes an exaggerated cackle. "But look at you now! Actually, I don't want to. We came to make sure you two didn't kill each other, but now I'm turning this car around." I hear her signal indicator clicking to demonstrate that she is, in fact, turning around. "Korra says she knew it too,"

"Well..." Zadie starts, still giggling and unable to say anything more.

"Actually," Korra says in the distance before taking the phone from her twin. "We were going to ask you about graduation. Nia's graduating in just over a month and when Kasey told me that you weren't home it's become this thing."

She meets my gaze and flushes slightly, "A thing it is," Zadie finally articulates, sitting up. "What about her graduation?"

"We're thinking of driving there together. Do you wanna come with?" Korra asks.

Zadie grins, "You know I am! I'd love to roadtrip with you all."

Korra clears her throat, "Since you and Lee have... whatever this is going on, do you think you could convince him to go?"

"I'll do my best," Red says, winking at me.

"Okay, ew," Kasey says. "Anyway, Zach and Gonzalo are going to fly since they can't miss that many days from the station. If you don't want to drive for whatever reason you can go with the guys, Lee."

My brows rise on my forehead. "Gonzalo is going? For what?"

"Well, isn't it obvious?" Zadie asks, tracing patterns on my thigh. I'll have time to get used to affection from her. For right now, I'm more than satisfied to be in awe of how languidly she touches me after all that has happened between us.

"No?" I scratch my head because I really don't see what reason Gonzalo would have for going to Tennessee to see my sister walk.

"Honestly, are you blind, little bro?" Kasey asks. "I guess that's your problem now, Zadie. I would criticize your taste in men, but considering that he's my brother—I'll give you a pass. But I have like, a million questions regarding this decision."

Of course, she does.

"Hey, mind your business. Don't call back," I say with a smirk before ending the call. There will be plenty of time for my sisters to give her hell.

Tonight, that's my job.

THE END

Thank You for Reading!

Thank you for joining me on this journey through Fierce Harmony. Your time and support mean the world to me, and I hope you've fallen in love with the characters and their story as much as I have!

Share Your Thoughts

If you enjoyed this book, leaving a review is one of the best ways to support authors like me. Reviews help other readers discover stories they'll love, and your voice matters! **Leave your review on Amazon or your favorite review site!**

Keep the Love Going

Perfect Harmony – An ambitious lawyer needs a fiancée to climb the ladder and his best friend agrees, but somewhere between the ring and their kiss, pretending starts to feel like the truth.

You can find all my books on my website: www.zeakayleighgalan.com

Stay Connected

Want to be the first to hear about new releases, exclusive content, and special offers?

Sign up for my newsletter at www.zeakayleighgalan.com/news

A Special Treat Just for You

Keep reading for an exclusive sneak peek at the previous book in the Thomas Family Saga series. Get ready to meet new characters, revisit familiar faces, and fall in love all over again. Thank you for being part of this journey. I can't wait to hear what you think!

Hugs, Zea Kayleigh Galan

Perfect Harmony Sneak Peek

KORRA

"That was tonight?"

I trail a line in the water between the cobblestones behind the club with my strappy heel while he shuffles around on the phone. Early fall rain has come and gone. Enough for it to cool the weather but not enough to skip on a good heel for a special night out.

Deep breath in.

As calm as I can manage, I remind him, "Today is my birthday. Of course, it was tonight."

Okay, maybe not as calm as I would have liked.

"Oh, Kor, it must have slipped my mind. I already brushed my teeth though. I'm not gonna be able to make it. We'll do something tomorrow night. Okay?"

I pick at a nail and immediately stop. I very rarely paint my nails anymore since they all chip off anyway. *This was a birthday treat.* Allowing him to ruin my manicure is not allowed.

"You have something planned?" I ask, filled with hope at the idea that he might have something better than a night clubbing to celebrate. He's the type...

I think.

"Not exactly—look it will be good. I promise." There's the trilling from his nightstand alarm clock that notes it's time for him to go to bed. "I gotta get to bed, so I can get up in the morning. You understand, right?"

"Yea..."

I thought he would have done something, anything, to celebrate me and I guess I was wrong. Maybe, I'm just expecting too much.

I look down at my phone, utterly dejected.

How does your own boyfriend forget your only birthday though?

Turning at the sound of the club door opening, my sister's best friend is standing there with a hand on her hip. "What are you doing out here? There's a whole party going on inside. You need to be in there!"

The harsh lighting from the street lamp illuminates Malaya's face beside the club's side entrance. I don't miss her look of concern.

Raising my phone for her to see it in my hand, I say, "You're so right. I was just on the phone with Palmer telling him good night."

She rolls her eyes. "Come on. That's enough of that." Malaya and Kasey both hate Palmer, but I know they just don't see him the way I do. *Outside of tonight*, he really is a good boyfriend.

The burly bouncer at the door steps aside to let us through. My friend never loosens her grip on my hand and she dances her way through the crowds and onto the dance floor. A perfect moment of all the moving bodies swaying more passionately when a hit song comes through the mix.

It feels good to let the swish of my hips move the fabric of my dress in a careless manner. I debated on wearing this dress tonight. The slinky forest green fabric is too nice for work and definitely too nice to get dirty on the weekend. But the club is the perfect place for me to show it off. Falling to a rhythm that heats my blood and makes it race, the smile on my face is genuine.

I'll be the first to admit that I prefer to be at home. This feeling is not one you can get in your living room though.

My friend raises our joined hands above our heads and we both dance to the beat with lights flashing and flickering over us. My spirits lift even higher as my sister comes to join us and then it's the three of us, belting the lyrics to the next song and then the next.

This is what I needed.

A carefree night with my girls and fruity cocktails that I don't have to watch because my brothers are here to make sure we get home safe.

Speaking of which, I search along the bar top tables at the far left for them. I spot Zach first since his hair is the biggest and he is the tallest. He looks around uncomfortably with a beer, I know he hasn't drank, in his iron-like grip. Lee is not looking too much more comfortable with his scowl on the dance floor scary enough to skin a cat with no tools.

When the sweat on my skin feels a little too dangerous to the carefully applied makeup I've chosen for tonight, I drag my sister and Malaya away from the dance floor and over to our table again.

Several men try to stop us on our way out. The shortest of the group, though he is probably the most attractive of the them, leans close to my ear to ask, "Can I buy you a drink?"

Palmer's face flashes in my mind and I say, "No, thank you though maybe my sister wants one." *I can at least be a good wing woman if nothing else.*

He doesn't seem deterred that I'm passing him off, but Kasey doesn't even let him try. Before he can open his mouth, she holds up a hand saying, "No," in capital letters.

Malaya doesn't let him get anywhere either with a quick point to the table we're headed towards. Lee is ready to jump over the balcony at this point. They bow out of the race, likely not wanting any of the smoke Lee is promising them with his glare.

I can't help but think—I should be pointing to Palmer over there. Or better yet, he should be here to ward off the advances to begin with.

I'm not single, but you'd never know it.

Kasey reaches the table first taking the seat next to Zach. I plop onto my stool, grabbing my rum and pineapple with fervor, downing what's left of it. I fan my face, "Why do they make these things so small? I'm going to melt. It's so hot in here." I lift my curls off my neck, trying to get some air flow back there.

"It's not meant to be gulped, you guppy. You ever heard of alcohol poisoning?" Lee chastises.

I stick my tongue out at him and casually scratch my nose with a middle finger painted boldly yellow. "Gee, thanks for that assessment, Doctor Dick. Just for that, I'm going to order two more. Have fun carrying me."

Lee rolls his eyes, "Yep, and I'll be sure to drop you off at home, so Dad can take care of his baby."

"Ah," I point at him, feeling victorious in catching his slip up. "Nia's not here. I'm the oldest at present."

"No, that would be me," Kasey corrects, primly drinking her sauvignon blanc. "By four minutes."

I wave her off. "We're twins, for argument's sake we're both the oldest."

"Got you both beat by four years," Zach says. "And I'm not carrying anyone home. Only rescues I do are from burning buildings and I'm off tonight."

I look to Malaya, "Please, tell your boyfriend that he is required to take us to our flat. That was the deal, right?"

She tilts her head from one side to the next. "Babe, I love you but you will not be cockblocking me tonight. I had a long day. Can't you get Palmer to do it?" She sips from her beer. It's not one of the light ones that Zach ordered for the table, but a dark stout. There is a moment of silence before she winces. "Sorry, I forgot. I mean what's up with that anyway?"

"What's up with what?" A deep, yet familiar voice asks from behind me.

I whirl, letting out a yelp as I hug my best friend. "You made it!" I yodel. It takes me a second, but I realize that I'm the only one embracing here. With my arms still around his neck, I ask, "Bryce, why aren't you hugging me back? Those are the birthday hug rules. Well, the hug rules, in general."

"Take a step back and you'd see," he says and I do just that.

Through slightly tipsy goggles, I look my friend over from top to bottom. His hair cut looks fresh, with the curls still in place on top and a taper up to his ears. Honestly, I think his curls are looking better than mine after all that dancing. He only has a slight shadow on his jaw from a shave this morning. His suit jacket is long gone, but he's wearing a pressed – actually more crumpled now from how tight I hugged him – button-down shirt and slacks. He must be coming from work and didn't change. I know for a fact that he owns casual clothes, clubbing clothes. These aren't them. His shoes are still shiny enough to reflect light by the time I make it there. "What am I seeing?"

His arms extend and I spot the light colored cocktail with the short black straw first. "Ooo, a—"

"Pineapple juice and rum, yea. And..." From behind his back he produces a brown paper bag and hands it to me.

"Um." I'm moments from shaking the bag before he stops me with a hand and an amused look. "What are you doing? Just open it."

"Right," I say, setting the drink down on the bar top. My sister catches my eye, but she says nothing with her lips twisted to the side and eyebrow raised. It's a look that tells me she's clocking something that I'm not. I *usually am not clocking what she's clocking though.*

Twin intuition fails me, yet again. I've got no idea what the face is for.

Using careful motions, I remove the sticker sealing the top and the tissue paper underneath. A whole heap of crinkled packing paper litters the club floor as I open the nondescript box in the bag.

With that out of the way, I catch the glint of the smooth glaze over crackle pottery.

"You didn't!" I yelp.

Everyone is leaning over the bar table to see what I'm making such a fuss about. I take a look around to show off how smug I am at the most perfect gift I've gotten this year.

Saying that isn't a big thing— Bryce gets the best gifts every year. Since I met him in the tenth grade, no one has ever topped him in that department. Not even Kasey and sometimes it's scary how well she can spot things. Don't get me wrong, her gifts are pretty great.

I don't know how he does it either. They're always the kind that make you think, "*Wow, I didn't know I needed this until you got it for me.*" Bryce takes the cake. Every time.

Carefully, I remove the pot from the box to show everyone what he purchased. I turn back to Bryce with all thirty-two teeth on display and the flash goes off.

I've come to expect his candid photos. Arguably, a gift in itself. He just has the natural ability to capture great moments. "Let me see," I say as he turns the phone around to show me. "Oh my goodness!" I bounce in my seat, "I look so good." Bryce and I look through the photos while my family is still trying to figure out exactly what my friend got me.

"Is that a cat?" Zach asks, with a shudder. He's got a bit of beef with them. Ever since a freak accident led to a broken arm. He had to save someone's neurotic cat who gave him grief in a rescue. Honestly, I didn't know why they send firefighters to help with those kinds of calls anymore. Most cats can get themselves down. They just don't want to.

"Awe, it's laughing," Malaya says from under Lee's arm. He looks completely unimpressed, but that's the little brother he is. I'm glad he isn't sharing a snarky remark because I would have to fight him.

Taryn's Pottery makes only small batches of these pots. The little cat's face looks paused in laughter. Excess water from the soil inside will drain through a small hole under the eyes that makes it look like the cat is literally cry-laughing. It's so niche and kitchy, but I love these pots. They cost way more than I can afford, especially for the one plant that I'm in a constant cycle of rehabilitating.

"This is the one, right?" Bryce asks, biting a corner of his lip. He scratches the back of his head. "You were always giggling at the videos. I didn't know if you just thought it was funny or if maybe I should have gotten the pig. I—"

"Ahh," I cut him off, placing the planter carefully onto the table next to my drink and jumping to hug him again. "It is purr-fect." I lean away from his chest since I barely reach, even in high heels, to look at him. "Get it? Get it cause..."

"You've been hanging around your brother too much," he says, shaking his head with a wide grin on his face. Lee is known for his animal puns. It started as him teasing our Dad because he thought they were cheesy and now he can't stop. Sometimes it's hard to take him serious when there is some hidden dog pun thrown into the mix. "Happy birthday," he says, finally releasing me from the hug. He looks around and then looks back at me. "Where is Palmer?"

Well shit. If Palmer has no haters, Malaya, Kasey and Bryce have all died. President of that hate-club is my best friend.

I grab my drink, murmuring into the straw, "He couldn't make it." Speaking as fast as possible, I add, "He's got work early, so he needs to rest tonight."

Bryce blinks once and then he blinks again. He raises a finger, mouth open to go off about my boyfriend but then lowers his hand. Patience is not my friend's forte. Especially not when it comes to Palmer.

Pinching his nostrils quickly and then deciding on, "He didn't take the day off? He's a dental assistant and it's," he checks his watch that catches the colorful club lighting. "Friday. I came right after being in court all day, several meetings and driving from the city." Bryce points across the club to the north, "He's right down the street!"

My drink is half gone, but he presses down on the glass until I let him return it to the table. Grumbling, I say, "Really thought you were gonna let it go..."

"Let. It. Go. You can't be serious." He looks at my sister, "Is she serious?"

Kasey is no help, adding, "I don't think she has been for a single day of her life. No."

I glare daggers at my brothers, they better not add to this ribbing.

"Hey! It's my birthday. Let's get back to the celebrations. I think the DJ is finally back to playing something I can break my back to!" For that I'm grateful. I need this subject change like an emergency exit right now.

Malaya finally gives me a life line to hold onto by agreeing that she'd like to dance, too.

"Sitting this round out," Kasey says, swirling what remains of her wine. "I'm ordering nachos."

Zach pipes up, "Make it three, sis."

She scans the little QR code on the table to pull up the ordering system. "Oh, good," Kasey looks at Zach, "It's on your tab already. I'll add some wings, too."

"Oldest privileges," he says, nursing that same beer. There might be more beer in the bottle than when I first spotted him from the dance floor.

"Good plan!" I say. Holding a hand out to Bryce, I ask, "May I have this twerk?" Exhibiting a move that absolutely would not qualify as twerking of any kind, Malaya joins in, mimicking my movements.

He chuckles though I know he's still pissed about Palmer. But, he can't resist my antics. "You may."

Continue reading Bryce and Korra's cozy friends-to-lovers, fake engagement story: **Perfect Harmony** here!

Acknowledgements

Here we are the end of Fierce Harmony or Lee and Zadie's story. Thank you so much for reading it and following on this journey through Harmony Hill again. It's wonderful to have you here, but also amazing to complete another piece of the Thomas Family Saga. I've spoken online about how enemies to lovers or rivals to lovers, in this case, is not a genre that I reach for, but it is such an appealing trope because that tension is irresistible. I went into their story hoping to deliver on the angst I'm known for, but kicking it up a notch by adding in that rivalry aspect. I'm so happy and proud of how their story unfolded. I hope you enjoyed it as well!

Thank you so much to my husband and daughter for being the support I need and the pillars that I pull my strength from. You two make me a better person just by being in my life. I love you!

Thank you to my PA, Kelsie! You keep this crazy train running! Your dedication to keeping me on track and helping our community keep up with all my chaos is commendable. In a lot of ways, this book came to be because you loved these characters even harder when I couldn't. Big, big squeeze!

Thank you to my BETA team for sticking beside me and offering your feedback and time. You are indispensable! Hugs!

Thank you to my ARC team for reading and sharing your reviews with friends and strangers alike! I know that you take care to highlight my stories and share your honest opinions online. Hugs!

Thank you to the Street team for working hard to share about this story and this series everywhere you can, as well as, encouraging others to try my work. Hugs!

Thank you again to you, the readers! Without you, I wouldn't be here to share my stories to begin with. I hope this story resonated with you and that you will join me for others in the future!

Never miss any future releases, events and extras from me by signing up to my newsletter:

https://zeakayleighgalan.com/news

Also by Zea Kayleigh Galan

Alpenglow Ridge

Saddled with Finesse – Can their unexpected kiss ignite a love strong enough to overcome the shadows of her past and give him the fresh start he's been searching for?

Verse to Acclimate – Years after heartbreak tore them apart, a broken small-town girl and country music's rising star must face the scars of their past to find out if love is worth a second chance.

Whisk til Peaked – Trapped by a snowstorm in a luxury resort with only one bed, a single mom and her loyal best friend must confront unspoken desires and buried secrets that could shatter everything they hold dear—or finally bring them together.

Hope by the Horizon – When a guarded hippotherapist clashes with charming ranch hand, their undeniable chemistry ignites a journey of trust, healing, and unexpected love—if they can overcome their pasts. (Read FREE https://zeakayleighgalan.com/free-novella)

Roped on the Ridge – She woke up with no memory, a past full of secrets, and a cowboy who refuses to give up on her... even when the truth threatens to destroy them both.

Shades of Vengeance

Into the Blue – A cold-hearted crime boss discovers that he can't let go of a dancer at his nightclub after she is attacked by his rival.

Written in Red – A dark stalker romance coming 2026!

Thomas Family Saga

Perfect Harmony – An ambitious lawyer needs a fiancée to climb the ladder and his best friend agrees, but somewhere between the ring and their kiss, pretending starts to feel like the truth.

Fierce Harmony – A lifelong rivalry gets complicated when a free-spirited woman and her best friend's brother are forced to choose between winning a shared dream or each other.

Sweet Harmony – A single-dad romance coming soon!

Made in the USA
Las Vegas, NV
17 February 2026

42075253R00128